The Higher Court

The Higher Court

Mary Stewart Daggett

MINT EDITIONS

The Higher Court was first published in 1911.

This edition published by Mint Editions 2020.

ISBN 9781513267654 | E-ISBN 9781513272658

Published by Mint Editions®

minteditionbooks.com

Publishing Director: Jennifer Newens
Design & Production: Rachel Lopez Metzger
Typesetting: Westchester Publishing Services

Chapter 1

Father Barry's late interview with his bishop had been short, devoid of controversy. Too angry to deny the convenient charge of "modernism," he sought the street. Personal appeal seemed futile to the young priest cast down by the will of a superior. To escape from holy, overheated apartments had been his one impulse. Facing a January blizzard, his power to think consecutively returned, while for a moment he faltered, inclined to go back. The icy air struck him full in the face as he staggered forward. "The only way—and one practically hopeless," he choked. Appeal to the archbishop absorbed his mind as he pressed on, weighing uncertain odds of ecclesiastical favor. Suddenly he realized that he had strayed from main thoroughfares, was standing on a desolate bluff that rose significantly above colorless bottom lands and two frozen rivers. Wind sharpened to steel, with miles of ceaseless shifting, slashed his cheeks, cut into his full temples, his eyes. He bowed before the gust so passionately charged with his own rebellion. To-day he was a priest only in name. For the first time since his assumption of orders he faced truth and a miserable pretense to Catholic discipline. Desires half forgotten stood out, duly exaggerated by recent disappointment. An impulse sent him close to the precipitous ledge, but he moved backward. To give up life was not his wish. He was defeated, yet something held him, as in a mirage of fallen hopes he saw a woman's face and cried out. He had done no wrong. Until the bishop cast him down he was confident, able to justify esthetic joy in ritualistic service, which took the place of a natural human tie. Now he knew that his work, after all, but expressed a woman's exquisite charm. For through plans and absorbing efforts in behalf of a splendid cathedral he had been fooled into thinking that he had conquered the disappointment of his earlier manhood. The bishop had apparently smiled on a dazzling achievement, and young Father Barry plunged zealously into a great undertaking. To give his western city a noble structure for posterity became a ruling passion, and in a few months his eloquence in the pulpit, together with unremitting personal labor on plans and elevations, had made the church a certainty. Thousands of dollars, then hundreds of thousands, fattened a building fund. The bishop appeared to be pleased; later he was astounded; finally he grew jealous and eager to be rid of the priest who swayed with words and ruled where a venerable superior made slight impression.

Consequently the charge of "modernism" fell like a bolt from a clear sky. Until to-day Father Barry had been absorbed in one idea. His cathedral had taken the place of all that a young man might naturally desire. When the woman he loved became free he still remained steadfast to his new ambition. It seemed as if lost opportunity had attuned his idealistic nature to symbolic love which could express in visions and latent passion an actual renunciation. That Isabel Doan understood and rejoiced in the mastery of his intellect gave him unconscious incentive. In the place of impossible earthly love he had awakened a consistent dream. Without doubt Mrs. Doan's pure profile was a motif for classic results. When he spoke to her of architectural plans, showing drawings for a splendid nave and superb arches, her keen appreciation always sent him forward with his work. Then, like true inspiration, visions came and went. Vista effects, altars bright with golden treasures stirred him to constant endeavor. He heard heavenly music—the best his young, rich city could procure. Day and night he worked and begged. Now all was over. For the second time in life the man faced hopeless disappointment. Deprived of work, removed from the large parish that for three years had hung on his every word and wish, the priest stood adrift in the storm. The ignominy of his downfall swept over him with every lash of an oncoming blizzard. He seemed to feel the end. The bishop's untethered brogue still clashed in his sensitive ears. The city he loved, now ready for the best of everything, no longer had a place for him. He was cast out. Below him spread bottom lands, dotted for miles with towering grain elevators, packing plants, and wholesale houses. Vitals of trade lay bare. By vivisection, as it were, he traced the life of commerce, felt gigantic heart beats of the lower town blending interests of two great states. In all directions rival railroads made glistening lines through priceless "bottoms." Father Barry groaned. Progress seemed to taunt his acknowledged failure. He turned his back. But again he faced promise. Higher ledges and the upper town retold a story of established growth. On every hand prosperity saluted him. Leading from bluffs, the city reached eastward for miles. As far as he could see domestic roof tops defined the course of streets. Houses crept to the edge of a retail district, then jumped beyond. On waiting acres of forest land splendid homes had arisen as if by magic. Through pangs of disappointment the priest made out the commanding site selected for his cathedral. A blasted dream evoked passionate prophecy, and the mirage of the church ordered and built by decrepit taste rose up before him. The bishop's unsightly work held him. Blinded by the storm, abnormally keen to a cruel delusion, he saw the end of his own laudable ambition. To his imagination, the odious brick box on the hillock seemed to be true. A commonplace elevation, with detached, square towers was real. With his brain maddened with hallucination, harsh, unmusical chimes began to sound above the blizzard's roar. Again and again he heard the refrain, "Too late! Too late!" The significance of a metallic summons almost stopped his breath, yet fancy led him on to the open church. He seemed to go within, pressing forward against the crowd. Below a flaming altar stood the bishop's bier. In the open casket, clad in robes of state, the old man slept the sleep of death. The brick monument to stubborn force echoed throughout with chanted requiem and whispered prayer. Incense clouded gorgeous vestments of officiating priests. Candles burned on every hand. At the Virgin's shrine flowers lent fragrance to an impressive scene. Then he seemed to forget the great occasion,—the bishop at last without power, the kneeling, praying throng. Longing for human love displaced all other feeling. In the image of one woman he beheld another, and Isabel Doan assumed the Virgin's niche.

Chapter 2

As the suspended priest went from the bluff the mirage of a few moments faded. The bishop still lived.

Reaction and the determination to face an archbishop impelled him forward. Why should he submit to sentence without effort to save himself? He drew the collar of his coat about his ears. At last he was sensitive to physical discomfort. Air sharp as splintered glass cut through his lungs. He bowed his head, revolving in his mind the definite charge of "modernism." What had he really said in the pulpit? Like all impassioned, extemporaneous speakers he could never quite recall his words when the occasion for their utterance had passed. Progress was undoubtedly his sinful theme; yet until lately no heretical taint had been found in the young father's sermons. Born a dreamer, reared a Catholic, he attempted rigid self-examination. The task proved futile. In Italy he would have led Catholic democrats in a great uprising. Despite the "Index" he rejoiced in the books of "Forgazzar." "Benedetto's" appeal to the pope to heal the "four wounds of Catholicism" clung to his mind. The great story touched him irresistibly. Sinful as it was, he had committed Benedetto's bold accusations to memory. "Il Santo" still drew him, and he was angry and sore.

He knew that in a moment of emotional uplift he had forgotten the danger of independent utterance, the bonds of a Catholic pulpit. But to-day, while he reverted to the sermon which had suspended him from the priesthood, he could not repeat one offensive sentence clearly.

The wind increased each moment. A blizzard of three days' duration might bring him time to think. At the end of the storm every one would hear of his suspension. The priest hurried on. Then he thought of his mother. Suddenly the dear soul had prior claim to Mrs. Doan. Above bitterness the son recalled the date; it was his thirty-second birthday. He told himself that nothing should keep him from the one who could best understand his predicament. This dear, sincere mother had counseled him before; why not now? The foolishness of troubling Mrs. Doan was clear. As he hastened on his way, he began to wonder what his mother would really think of the bishop's action. Would she accept her son's humiliation with serene, unqualified spirit? Would her faith in a superior's judgment hold? The suspended priest felt the terms for the true Catholic. He dreaded palliation of the bishop's course. But no—his mother could never do that. In the case in question her boy must stand injured, unjustly dealt with.

Father Barry went on with definite intention. His present wish was to spend a fatal birthday in the home of his boyhood. Fortunately, it was Monday. Father Corrigan had charge of weekly services. The younger man's absence would not be construed until after the blizzard. It flashed through his mind that on the coming Sunday he had hoped to make the address of his life. Now this last appeal in behalf of a great cathedral would never be uttered. On his study desk were plans and detail drawings which must soon cumber a waste basket. Suddenly the young priest, cast down, humiliated, turned from the tents of his people, longed to cry out to hundreds who loved him—who believed in him. But again his thoughts turned to his mother, who would soon hold him in her loving arms, cry with him, beg him to be patient, worthy of his bringing up. Then he knew that he was not a true Catholic. His binding vows all at once seemed pitiless to his thwarted ambition and human longing.

Chapter 3

When Father Barry reached the parsonage he found no use for a pass key. Pat Murphy, his faithful servant and acolyte, was watching for him just within the door. He drew the half-frozen priest across a small entry, to a large warmed apartment answering to-day as both study and dining-room. "The rist of the house do be perishing," the Irishman explained. The priest sank in front of a blazing coal fire, tossing his gloves to the table. He held his hands before the glow without comment. They were wonderful hands, denoting artistic temperament, but with fingers too pliant, too delicately slender for ascetic life. Philip Barry's hands seemed formed for luxury, and in accordance with their expression he had surrounded himself with both comfort and chaste beauty. In the large, low, old-fashioned room in which he sat there was no false note. Pictures, oriental rugs, richly carved chairs—all represented taste and expenditure, somewhat prejudicial to a priest's standing with his bishop. That the greater part of everything in the little house had arrived as a gift from some admiring parishioner but added to the aged superior's disapproval of esthetic influence. To-day Father Barry warmed his hands without the usual sense of comfortable home-coming. Pat Murphy observed that for once his master showed no interest in a row of flower boxes piled on the table.

"Will you not be undoing your birthday presents?" the Irishman ventured. The priest turned his back to the fire. "I must get warm. I am frozen to the bone," yet he moved forward. One box held his eye like a magnet. He knew instinctively that Isabel Doan had remembered his anniversary. Unmindful of all other offerings, he broke the string and sank his face into a bed of ascension lilies. He seemed to inhale a message. His eyes felt wet. Pat Murphy brought him back to earth. The acolyte stood at his elbow. "May I not bring water for the posies?" he humbly begged. Father Barry frowned. "Untie the other flowers; I will attend to these myself." He surveyed the room, at last, reaching for an ample jar of dull-green pottery. The effect was marvelous. Like the woman who had sent them, the lilies stood out with rare significance. The priest glanced again into the empty box, searching for the friendly note which never failed to come on his birthday. As he supposed, the envelope had slipped beneath a bed of green. He broke the seal, then read:

My dear Father Barry:

How shall you like the settled-down age of thirty-two? Are we not both growing old and happy? I am thinking constantly of your splendid work, and have sent with the lilies a little check for the new cathedral. I pray that you will permit a poor heretic to share in your love for art. Do as you think best with the money—yet if some personal wish of yours might stand as mine—a beautiful window perhaps?—I should feel the joy of our joint endeavor.

But remember, the check is yours to burn in a furnace or to pay out for stone. You will know best what to do, and in any case, the poor heretic may still hope for a bit of indulgence from St. Peter. Meantime, I am coming to hear you preach. When I tell you that I fear to have a young Catholic on my hands, you will not be surprised that Reginald teases each week to go to Father Barry's pretty church. He admires your vestments with all his ardent little soul. Unfortunately at present my dear boy has a miserable cold and a bad throat. I am thinking of taking him to Southern California for the winter. Before our departure I shall hope to see you.

With kindest wishes for a happy birthday, I am always your friend.

Isabel Chester Doan

The note was dated two days back, and the enclosed check stood for three thousand dollars. Father Barry bowed his head. Again his eyes were wet. When Pat importuned him to come to luncheon, he sat down with unconquerable emotion. He could not endure the ordeal, so pushed away his plate.

"If ye don't be tasting mate, ye'll be fainting," Pat insisted. The priest smiled miserably. "Don't worry—I'm only tired. Besides, I'm going to my mother; she will see that I need coddling. Pack my case; I wish to start at once."

The acolyte scanned the pile of boxes.

"The pink carnations I shall give to mother; the other flowers you may carry to the hospital. Go as soon as possible," the master commanded. "Tell Sister Simplice to see that each patient has a posey. The fruit I send to old Mrs. Sharp. Explain that her confessor orders white grapes in place of a penance."

"And the lily flowers—do I be taking them to the hospital, too?"

"No," the priest answered. "In no case meddle with the lilies." He moved the jar to a position of honor on top of his desk. "These will remain fresh until I return. Do not touch them or let them freeze." He leaned forward with caressing impulse; then his eyes fell hard and sober on parchment rolls and detail drawings. Cherished plans for his cathedral, plans now useless, lay piled before him. He closed his secretary.

"If any one calls—say that I am from home—on business. I must not be pursued."

Murphy grinned. "I'm on to the thrick! And it's not a day for resaving visitors." A prolonged gust made his words plausible. Father Barry tried to smile.

"You are a good fellow, Pat. Should I never come back—confess to Father Corrigan." The priest's mood was difficult. As the Irishman watched his adored master charge into the blizzard he frowned perplexedly. "He do run like Lot afeared of Soddom," he exclaimed. "But it's sick he is—nadin rist at his mother's. Warkin' day and night on his cathedral has all but laid him low." Pat poked the fire. "Mike, up at the bishop's, do be sayin' nasty things. And sure, 'tis nothin' but foolishness, surmisin' how the old bishop do be atin' out his heart on account of a young praste's handsome face and takin' ways. Mike be cursed for a Jesute, startin' scandal from a kayhole!" He picked up the coal hod. "I must kape his lily posies as he bid me." He pressed close to a frosted window. Through a clear spot in the glass he could see his master breasting the storm. "He's all but off his feet," he muttered.

Murphy was Father Barry's own delightful discovery. Months back the priest had engaged the raw Irish boy for household service, then later promoted him to a post of honor about the altar. To faithful Pat there was little more to ask for outside of heaven. Reports which he sent home to Ireland were set down on paper by Mike, who served in the upper household. Pat's scribe published his friend's felicity broadcast, until at length even the bishop was fully informed of a popular young priest's affairs. Without thought of injury to one whom he adored, Pat extolled the plans for the great cathedral, which possibly might eclipse St. Peter's at Rome. Again and again the boy dwelt on Father Barry's popularity. To-day as the acolyte looked through the frost-glazed window, scratching wider range with his thumb nail, he had no doubt of his master's chance to become a prelate. Soon the "old one" would pass beyond. He crossed himself devoutly, peering hard at the tall, retreating form, now almost within reach of the corner. An electric line but half a block away was Father Barry's goal. As Pat looked, a gust sent the pedestrian onward with a plunge. As usual, the master carried his own suit case. Murphy muttered disapproval. At the crossing the priest stopped to regain his breath. His sole wish was to catch a car. Owing to the blizzard, traffic might suspend; but in the wind-charged air he thankfully detected a distant hum. The trolleys yet ran. How fortunate! And now very soon he would be with his mother—practically lost to a storm-bound community. How sweet the shelter waiting. Soon he might unburden his heart—pour out his trouble before the only woman in the world who would really understand it. Then again he remembered Isabel Doan—her check, the letter hiding against his breast. After all, should he not restore the generous gift at once? Now that the original cathedral could not be built, was it not a matter of personal honor to explain? Altered conditions cancelled both his own and his friend's obligation. Mrs. Doan must take back her check. That the bishop was powerless to claim the donation filled the priest with vindictive joy. Gradually duty to his mother ceased to govern him. Beyond everything else he wanted to see Isabel Doan. He told himself that he had a right to do so. Honeyed sophistry provided motive for his desire. He stood, as it were, at a point defined by opposing ways. Double tracks glistened before him; one leading eight blocks distant to the lintel of his mother's door; the other, stretching in the opposite direction, across the city—almost to a certain stone mansion. The priest was not in a mood of valiant resistance. Again he longed for Isabel Doan's sympathy. Yet, as he tarried at the crossing, waiting, still undecided which line to choose, he could not dismiss the thought of his mother, even now, watching for her son. He could fancy the dear lady sitting by the window, expectant, disappointed when no car stopped. Her sweet flushed face; the adorable white hair parted and waved on each side of a forehead gently lined by time made a picture which he could not easily dismiss. This mother was his ideal of age. She seemed as rare, as beautiful as an exquisite prayer-rug grown soft and precious with mellow suns and golden years. Many times he had contrasted her with overdressed, elderly women of his parish. He had never wished her to be different in any respect.

He would go to her now. She would tell him what to do; and after dinner, when the dear lady was thinking of early bedtime, he might slip away with Isabel Doan's check. He must return it in person. He shifted from one foot to the other and beat his arms across his breast. The charge of the blizzard was paralyzing. Down the way a car was coming—a red one, he was sure of it—glad of it. His mother would be waiting for him. For the time he forgot a parallel track and that other destination directly west. Suddenly like songs of sirens, he heard the buzz of opposing trolleys. Two cars would meet before his eyes! But the red one still led. Yet how strange: it had just stopped. The yellow opponent came on. The priest breathed hard. Fate seemed to be thrashing his will with the storm. Again the red car moved and the yellow one halted. Chance was playing a game. He leaned expectant from the curb. Something had gone wrong, for once more the red line had lost the trolley, then an instant later a yellow car stood on the crossing. Father Barry sprang over the tracks, veered around to an open side, jumped aboard.

Chapter 4

Once within the east-bound car the suspended priest found valid excuse for what he had done. Even now he need not disappoint his mother. As soon as he reached the house of Mrs. Doan he could telephone the dear soul, explain that urgent business detained him. By dusk he would be free, ready to pour out his heart to the best woman in the world. In case the increasing storm should interfere with the cars, there was always a hansom cab at a nearby stable. His forethought pleased him; and again he told himself that the present course of action was justified.

To return Mrs. Doan's generous check—simply as he might return it to any friend who trusted him—was sufficient motive for either priest or man. He settled comfortably in an empty seat; then felt in the breast of his inside coat for Isabel's letter. The straightforward wording appealed to him even more than at first. How like this woman to put aside prudery. How like her to wish to bestow through art a gift denied by love. And she was soon going away—to far California—with the little son whom she fairly adored. There was no place in her pure affection for any man. The boy seemed to be all that she asked for. He frowned, putting away the note. For several moments he blankly gazed through the window. With the certainty of his undoing, he again blamed the bishop for all that was sinful to the soul of a priest. He felt that he had lost his religion forever. Beads of perspiration stood on his forehead. He was bitter, bitter. An hour before he had believed that he could find courage and intellectual ability to lay his case before an archbishop; but now all was changed. He no longer desired to remain a priest. Exalted sentiments were not to his credit when lip service made them detestable. He felt no terror at the thought of excommunication. As soon as he was man enough to tell the truth he might be free. Still, with a last desperate confession could he ever rise from ignominy? Where should he find refuge? Perhaps in his knowledge of architecture, and he might write books. The elastic hope of an artistic temperament lured him, until suddenly he once more remembered his mother. How could he slay this trustful, simple soul? As the car sped across the city his mind turned to his childhood, his boyhood, his early manhood.

Ever since he could remember, he had been everything to his dear mother. When he was but a baby a scourge of cholera had taken away his father. Several years later a beautiful sister died, and finally a grown brother. Then Philip had become the widow's sole companion. The Irish lady, of gentle blood, alone in a strange land—fortunately a kind one—thought only of her little son. Soon the lad swung a censer before the church altar, while shortly his mother was termed wealthy by reason of wise investments and increasing values. Philip enjoyed judicious indulgence. The devout Catholic lived but for her son and her religion. Early in life she taught the boy to accept without question the authority of his Church. For a lad of poetic, emotional temperament, the duty of service fraught with certain reward seemed easy. Philip loved everything connected with his own little part in the chancel. The impressive latin chanted by priests clad in gorgeous robes fired his imagination, made him long to understand, to become versed in a mysterious tongue. High Mass had always been dramatic, something to enjoy, exalted above play and mere physical exercise. Voices floating from the choir sounded like angels. The boy adored the high soprano and enshrined her in his imagination with the gold-crowned Virgin. St. Joseph did not interest him, but he spent much time admiring the yellow curls of Mary. Young girls with bright hair stole his heart. He associated all beautiful women with the Virgin. His little sweethearts invariably ruled him with shining, tossing curls of gold.

Then at last the lad gave up attendance at the altar, laid aside his lace-trimmed cotta to depart for college. During four successful years the watchful mother felt no change in her son's religious nature; but the shock came. When he returned from an extended trip abroad she saw at once that something had influenced him to question the authority of his Church. The visit to Rome had not strengthened Philip's faith. He had become indifferent about confession. Often he was critical of officiating priests. Then one day the mother understood the full measure of her son's backsliding. All at once he poured out his heart—told defiantly of his love for a girl not a Catholic. The poor lady knew the worst, knew that Philip had been with Isabel Chester in Italy. However, the mother's terror and anxiety were both of short duration. Miss Chester's family interfered almost at once, and soon the young woman who had threatened the soul of Philip Barry became the wife of another man.

As time went by the zealous faith of the widow was rewarded, for one day Philip expressed the wish to retire to a monastery. The decision brought happy tears to the deluded mother's eyes. Her boy's emotional nature did not disturb her own simple faith. Philip was saved. But she asked for more, and more came. When her son was duly consecrated to the Catholic priesthood the event stood out as the greatest day in her life.

The young man's later career, his brilliancy, his popularity, even his dream of the cathedral, were all as nothing to the real cause of his mother's joy. In all the woman's years she had never doubted a syllable of her faith. To give her son wholly to her Church was a privilege so sweet that to lose it at last might take away her life. Again everything flashed through the mind of the priest verging on apostacy. He bowed his head. Could he go through with his awful part—forget his mother? From the car window he saw tall, naked elms a block away. A corner near the home of Mrs. Doan was almost reached. Behind denuded trees stood the stone house of the woman he wished to see. Questions scarcely faced were left unanswered as he jumped from the car. A rushing gust almost knocked him down, but he righted himself and pressed forward. Piercing air cut into his lungs; the blizzard with all its sharp, mad frenzy had arrived. Above, the sky, clear, electrical, was a sounding dome for oncoming blasts. Wings of wind beat him onward. He fought his way with labored breath. Naked elms, chastised by the gale, motioned him; and plunging, he reached the vestibule to Mrs. Doan's tightly closed door.

Chapter 5

The door opened on a city official. "You can't come in; we've got a case of diphtheria," he exclaimed. "I'm ready to placard the house."

Father Barry pushed forward. "I go in at my own risk—do not try to stop me. These people are my friends; they are in trouble—I must see them."

He passed by the officer, into a wide hall. Maggie Murphy, Pat's cousin, and Reginald Doan's devoted nurse, met him with swollen, streaming eyes. "Good Father!" she sobbed, "will you not say prayers for our darlin'? He's that sick, 'tis all but sure we must give him up." In her excitement the girl spoke with native brogue.

"Be quiet," the priest implored. "This is no time for tears. You must keep yourself in hand. Remember the boy's mother and do your part in a tranquil way."

Maggie made the sign of the cross, then led her confessor to the library, where Mrs. Grace, a carefully preserved woman of middle age, greeted him with outstretched hands. Isabel Doan's aunt had been weeping too, but judiciously. When she perceived Father Barry a desire to appear her best effaced lines of grief.

"Dear, dear Father!" she faltered. "How very good of you to come. How did you know?" She pressed an exquisite Roman crucifix to her lips; for unlike her niece, Mrs. Grace was a Catholic.

"I heard only when I reached the door," the priest admitted.

"A short time ago we thought our darling would die; but now there is the slightest hope that we may keep him. His mother is wild with suspense." The lady wiped her eyes. "We can do absolutely nothing with Isabel. She refuses to leave Reggie's room, even for a moment. I am sure she has not closed her eyes since yesterday."

"The doctor must send her to bed at once," said the priest.

"Both he and the nurse have tried to do so, but she will not go. I believe she would die if Reggie should be taken. O dear Father, will you not say prayers?"

Mrs. Grace sank to her knees, wrapt and expectant. Maggie Murphy flopped audibly in the hall, while for Philip Barry the moment was fraught with indecision. He seemed to think in flashes. He wanted to cry out, to publish himself, to deny the very garb he wore. Then the next instant he longed to entreat for the life of Isabel Doan's boy. The sweeter side of his profession held him. After all, what difference did it make if he might give comfort to women in distress? The prayers of notorious sinners had been answered on the spot. Why should not he, the vilest of hypocrites, yet honest for the time, ask for the life of a dying boy? He felt for his priest's prayerbook. Fortunately he had not changed his coat since his rude awakening. The little book he always carried was still in his breast pocket, fairly touching Mrs. Doan's letter and enclosed check. He found the place and began. His knees trembled, but his voice came strong and clear. A last opportunity had nothing to do with what might follow; this one moment was between God and his own conscience. Tenderness thrilled throughout him as he went on with familiar prayers. In the hall Maggie Murphy's sobs made passionate refrain for his importunate pleading; then instinctively he felt the presence of Isabel, knew that she stood behind him. He rose from the floor and faced her. She answered his unspoken question with a smile. "He is better. The doctor thinks the anti-toxin has saved him." In all his life Philip Barry had never seen such joy on a woman's face.

Mrs. Grace sprang from her knees. "Is Reggie really better? really better?" she repeated. Her intensity jarred.

Isabel smiled. "We think so," she answered. "Of course the doctor cannot tell just yet. Complications might occur; but he hopes!" Again her face was radiant.

Mrs. Grace crossed herself.

"The membrane in the throat is quite broken," Mrs. Doan went on. "The anti-toxin worked wonderfully. Now we can only wait."

"And *you* should take needed rest," the priest put in impulsively. He seemed to have the right to dictate to this woman in trouble. For as he stood by Isabel's side he began to realize how absolutely over were the once serious relations of their lives. The two might be friends—nothing else. Mrs. Doan had no thought for a priest other than exalted friendship. An accepted lack in her married life made it natural for her to bestow exquisite love on her child. That which she had not been able to give her husband she now dispensed to his son. The boy filled her heart. "You will take needed rest?" Father Barry again entreated, when Mrs. Grace, frank and always tactless, bemoaned the wan appearance of her niece.

"Do go to bed, Isabel; make up your lost sleep," the lady urged. "You are a ghost! I never saw you looking worse. Those dark circles below your eyes make you ten years older."

The older woman's crudeness stood out in marked contrast with her careful toilet. Anxiety had not deprived Mrs. Grace of either rest or studied accessories.

Isabel shook her head. "I could not sleep," she answered. "When the assistant nurse arrives I shall have less responsibility; but until then I must stay with Reggie. My darling's eyes are always hunting for me. You know I wear a masque, the doctor insists upon it; and when I cross the room my dear little boy cannot feel quite sure about his mother. But now I have braided my hair and tied the ends with blue ribbon. The nurse is just my height, and we both wear white." She glanced down at her summer frock, brought from the attic for sudden duty. "Reggie will know me by my colors."

Her pure garb, together with ropes of golden hair falling down from a part, made saintly ensemble. Once before—in Rome—the priest had seen her as she looked to-day. Then, too, dark circles deepened the violet of her wonderful eyes. As now, she had felt miserable, in doubt. The man who denied a selfish part in an unforeseen moment was suddenly conscious of his deadly sin. But now he prayed, asking for strength divorced from pretense. And at last he believed that his main thought was a desire to help an afflicted household, a wish to support friends in time of need. He told himself that he might give Reginald Doan personal care simply as he had done before for other children less precious, less beautiful; for apart from the mother Father Barry loved her boy.

Chapter 6

Throughout night the blizzard raged. Traffic was suspended; no one ventured into the streets on foot. The assistant nurse did not arrive, and with quickened pulse but masterful will Philip Barry assumed her place in the sick child's chamber. Isabel had been persuaded to retire. At midnight the terrific force of the storm brought her below to the library. She could not sleep, but sat in a chair by the fire, somewhat comforted. Oak logs made grateful glow for the mother scarce able to resist the temptation to fly to her boy. But she had promised to keep away. In case she was needed she would be sent for.

In her restless state she could not endure to be alone, and rang for Maggie. The faithful girl reported at once, while together the two made ready a tray for Reginald's night watchers. Longing for action, Isabel prepared hot chocolate with her own hands. A cold bird, rolls, and jelly completed a tempting repast. The maid carried up the little supper, her mistress waiting anxiously until she came back radiant with good news.

"He's better, mam—the darlin's much better!" Maggie crossed herself. "Father Barry beats the doctor! Nurse says Reggie minds him wonderful, not even fretting for you. Now do be going back to a warm bed."

Isabel shook her head. "I would rather stay here," she answered. "The wind sounds so loud from my room. Put on a log; I shall toast, sleep in my chair."

"If you don't mind I'll stay with you," the girl implored.

"That will not be necessary. You had better go; to-morrow you may be needed."

Maggie moved reluctantly from the room, as Mrs. Doan dropped into the depths of her chair. The fire sent out a soft, protecting glow, touching her face with hope. In flowing robe, with unbound braids, she seemed like a Madonna dreaming of her child. Soon she slept. Wind, plunging against the windows, shrieking disappointment, wasting its demon's force in plaintive wail, no longer disturbed her. Hours passed while she rested. Something she did not try to explain had happened; the burden of doubt, of crushing responsibility seemed to be lifted. Her aunt's incompetence, the excited maids praying about, were forgotten. Help had come from an unexpected source; and stranger than anything else she had been willing to accept it.

And Father Barry, caring for the sick child, felt corresponding peace. He was once more a priest in active service. It seemed right, natural, that he should assume his present place. In all his life he had never felt so strong, so uplifted. Bitter feelings of the day were gone, dismissed under incessant pressure and critical conditions. To save the boy was his only thought. He rejoiced in service, more than ever before seemed to feel the worth of humility. It came over him that to accept his suspension, to respect the will of his superior and go into temporary seclusion, might after all be best. He thought of days in a monastery almost with longing. Once before he had sought shelter with good men who knew how to obey. In his first boyish sorrow quiet had brought him relief. In routine even in mild hardship, he had believed that he had discovered a world outside of self. He now hoped that a period of self-examination with solitude would set him right, fit him for the priest's part he had chosen. Then Reginald Doan held out his tiny hands imploring help. The man took him in his arms and held him, and the little one found comfort. For an hour Father Barry listened to the boy's breathing with renewed hope. When the nurse came the child was sleeping. She smiled, but ordered her patient beneath the covers of the bed.

"If you do not mind, please see about the furnace. Williams may have dropped off. We must take no chance on a night like this. The slightest change in temperature would ruin all we have done." She bent over the boy in watchful silence while the priest went out. At the top of the staircase he took off his shoes. He held one in each hand, treading softly to the hall below. The house gave forth the intense quiet of night, but between the library curtains a stream of light lured him onward. It was his part to guard the house from accident, and he ventured into the room; then stopped, powerless to retreat. Isabel Doan slept in her chair. Her rare face, touched with ineffable peace, shone in profile against dark cushions. She seemed a modeled relief. Gentle breathing moved no fold of her loosely gathered robe; not even her unbound hair stirred ever so lightly. Oblivion claimed the mother, half ill from exhaustion. Close to the hearth a pair of tiny slippers rested motionless. The priest tarried, sinning within his heart. It was but a moment—yet long enough. Suddenly he knew that everything was changed. Isabel was no longer for him, nor he for her. Their divergent lives could never come together. He shrank from the room, not looking back. To escape without disturbing the sleeper impelled him into the very cellar; then he sank to the floor—to his knees. For the second time since entering the house he prayed as a priest. Deliverance from self was the burden of his cry. In his deplorable state he seemed adrift in the dark. He might be neither man nor priest. There was now no place for him in the world he had tried to forsake, nor could he longer fulfill the false part in his mistaken calling. An opening door restored his composure, for despite his emotional nature Philip Barry knew well the cooler demand of time and place. He spoke to the man in charge of the furnace, then examined the gauge. "Not a fraction of a degree must be overlooked," he ordered peremptorily.

"And the boy?" said the man.

"Better. Everything from now on depends on ourselves. I came below to satisfy the nurse. She cautioned me to say that the slightest change in temperature would be fatal to her little patient."

As the priest spoke he turned about. Again he put away everything but the one object which detained him in Mrs. Doan's house. To nurse her boy through a terrible night, then to go out—forever—from temptation he could not meet was his only thought.

Chapter 7

Night wore on. By morning the passion of the storm was abated. The blizzard had not lifted; but waves of wind burst less frequently on a world now white with frozen snow.

Early in the day the doctor arrived with the belated nurse. The priest was virtually discharged from duty. He would have gone away at once but for Reginald, who held tightly to his hand. The sick boy was sweetly despotic in his little kingdom. A child's appealing trust, his angelic weakness, claimed all that Father Barry could give. "Reggie—won't have—nudder nurse," he protested. The young woman who had just arrived moved into the background, while the boy's mother sank to his side. Isabel's face shone with joy. The gladness of the moment half stopped her voice. But she took her darling's tiny hand. Reginald's fingers clung to her own; then, with a satisfied smile, he reached out eagerly to the priest. "Hold nudder hand," he implored. To refuse was not to be thought of. Father Barry knelt once more; but now, like a jewel in a clasp, the precious body of the boy joined him to Isabel. On opposite sides of the bed, both man and woman felt instant thrill of a despotic measure. The sick child's eyes sought eagerly for his new nurse. "You can go home," he announced. "Take your trunk," he coolly added. He sighed contentedly, looking first at his mother, then at his friend. The French clock on the dresser ticked moments. The boy seemed to be asleep. He was only planning fresh despotism. "Mudder dear and Fadder Barry will make Reggie well," he summed up conclusively. "Some day—I'm doin' to buy Fadder Barry a wotto-mobile—a nice, bu-ti-ful—great big one——"

"Thank you," said the priest. The child spoke easily. His improvement seemed marvelous.

"Dear Reggie must not talk. Be quiet, darling," Isabel entreated. "Mother dear and Father Barry will both stay with you; but you must close your eyes and go to sleep." Unconscious of the priest's emotion the mother had promised much. The boy drooped his lids, squeezing them hard. Below purple eyes, dark lashes swept his cheeks, then raised like curtains, as he peeped on either hand. Isabel was faint with joy.

"Darling," she pleaded, "go to sleep."

"I can't keep shut," the little fellow whimpered. His head turned on the pillow. "I want Fadder Barry to put on his fine cape and his nice suit," he begged, suddenly recalling the priest's vestments. "And I want to hear the little bell," he persisted.

"Yes, dear Reggie," Father Barry answered. "When you are well you may come to church—may hear the beautiful music—see the little boys about the altar. But now you must mind the doctor. Don't you remember? just a little time ago you told him that you would be a good boy and do everything Father Barry wished. If you talk your throat will get bad again. You don't want it to hurt?"

Sympathy wrought on the boy's imaginative temperament; he enjoyed his own little part. "I felt so bad!" he wailed. He had naturally a broad accent, despite his Middle West locality. His voice, deep and full for so young a child, inclined to unflattened vowels.

"I felt so bad!" he repeated, in view of more attention.

"But now you will soon be well," his mother quieted. "Just think how good you should be when you are going to California!"

The promise in question acted like magic.

"Tell Reggie about the big ningen," he coaxed.

"If you close your eyes," Isabel agreed. The boy's lashes shut down. "Soon mother dear and Reggie are going far away on a long train," she began. "Every morning the engineer will give his big engine a hot breakfast,—a great deal of coal, and all the water it can drink. The long, long train will run ever so fast, away out across the plains, over the high mountains, to California. At first Jack Frost may try to catch the train, but the engineer must run the faster. Then soon Jack Frost will go howling back East."

"I want Fadder Barry to come too," the boy put in.

"If you talk, I shall not go on," his mother cautioned. "Reggie may eat his breakfast and dinner and supper on the train. At night he will sleep in a funny little bed. Maggie must watch that her boy doesn't roll on to the floor. After a long time the train will stop. Mother and Reggie and Maggie will get out, and——"

"Fadder Barry, too!" the boy persisted. He did not open his eyes, while tremulous lashes expressed his joy in the story.

"When Reggie gets to California he won't have to wear mittens or carry his muff or put on his fur coat," the mother continued, regardless of comment. "It will be bright and warm, so warm that Reggie may play out of doors all day long. There will be gardens filled with flowers. Mother's little boy may pick her a beautiful bouquet every morning."

"And Fadder Barry, too—and Maggie—and——" The sick boy was reluctantly dropping to sleep. The rhythm of his mother's voice and a satisfying story had worked a charm.

"In California the trees are full of birds that sing just like Dickey; only poor Dickey has to live in his cage. In California the birds are free to fly. Sometimes they fly over the great mountains; sometimes down to the deep, big ocean." The boy's dark lashes had ceased to quiver. "All day long yellow bees and bright butterflies play hide and seek among the flowers; at night they all go to bed inside of roses, tucked between pink and white blankets, just like little boys and girls. They sleep—and sleep—and sleep—just like Reggie."

The priest and Isabel looked into each other's eyes. For a moment they held the tiny fingers of the boy, then very gently each released a hand and moved from the bedside.

The nurse came forward, smiling. "You might both better go," she commanded. Without comment the boy's mother led the way. In the hall below, Pat Murphy stood in earnest conversation with his cousin Maggie. The girl looked frightened. Father Barry approached without hesitation. "What is the matter?" he asked.

The Irishman waited, confused. "I do be sint by Sister Simplice. Your mother—the old lady—she have just gone." He crossed himself.

"Tell me again," the priest commanded. "What do you mean?"

"Your mother—do be dead," Pat faltered.

Chapter 8

"She has been gone an hour," said Sister Simplice.

Father Barry followed the nun, half dazed, to the upper hall, for as yet he could not grasp the force of his own miserable, late arrival. Outside the closed door of his mother's room he waited.

"Tell me all!" he implored. "I must know the worst—before I see her. Tell me everything; what she said at the very last." His voice broke into sobs as he dropped to a couch.

Sister Simplice drifted to his side. Her words were low and calm; only her delicate profile, with slightly quivering nostrils, expressed agitation. She looked straight beyond; not at the closed door. Like one rehearsing a part she began to speak. Father Barry's head sank forward into his hands. The nun's story fell gently, mercifully softened. As she went on the priest raised his eyes. Sister Simplice dreaded the question burning on his lips.

"And she did not believe that I had neglected her—forgotten to come to her on my birthday?"

"She thought no ill of her son," the nun answered. "When I came last night the danger of her first sudden attack seemed to be over. She had rallied, was perfectly conscious. 'He will come in the morning, when the storm is over,' she told us at midnight. 'Yes,' I said, 'he will surely come. Day will bring him safe from his hiding place.'"

Father Barry bowed his head.

"You remember that you telephoned in the early afternoon? The storm had already interfered with service. She could not catch your words, felt only that you were detained upon some errand of mercy. When Pat Murphy brought the flowers to the hospital he said nothing whatever of your movements. This morning he happened to come with your mail, just after the dear one passed away. I sent him out to find you." The priest wept softly. "We had no thought of the end when it came," the nun went on. "So quickly, so peacefully, she left us. She seemed to be much better with the dawn, for the storm that kept you from her side had abated. She was expecting you every moment. She had no thought of death." Sister Simplice crossed herself. "Faithful Nora had brought a cup of nourishment, we were about to offer it, when, brightening like her old self, she begged for a fresh shawl."

"I understand," the priest faltered. "She wished to look neat and charming. And it was all for me!" he burst out. "She wanted me to find her as usual—like her pretty self."

"Yes," the nun answered, "she asked for a shawl you admired—the one with a touch of lavender. Nora brought a white cape from the closet, but she motioned it away. 'I wish my fine new shawl, the one my son likes best,' she pleaded. We were gone from the bedside but a moment, both searching in the closet. Your dear mother was unconscious, almost gone, when we returned."

Sister Simplice crossed herself again. The priest could not speak. Stillness followed the nun's story; only the ticking of a clock disturbed his pent thoughts. Suddenly the man burst forth as a boy.

"I should have come to her sooner!" he confessed. "I knew that she had not been well the week before; but I thought her slight attack was from the stomach. How could I dream of this! She assured me that she felt like herself, and the morning of my birthday"—he hesitated—"the morning of my birthday I was compelled to go to the bishop."

"Yes," the nun interrupted—"she understood—knew how you were working for the cathedral. Her pride in your success was beautiful. She asked for no hour which justly belonged to the service of your Church."

"Thank God! she never knew—died believing in me—thought I had succeeded," the priest cried passionately. The nun lifted her crucifix.

"The blessed saints ordained that she should think nothing but good of her son—her priest—her one earthly idol." Sister Simplice clasped her hands. "Have no fear for her soul. A soul—such as hers—must rise freed from transient torment. Soon she will follow from afar—follow her son's great earthly work." Father Barry groaned.

"You do not understand; do not know that I am almost glad that my mother has gone—passed safely beyond. She was a good Catholic. If she had lived—" he rose to his feet and stood before the trembling sister—"if she had lived to know the truth she might have rebelled, have doubted."

The sister flushed, then turned pale. Nun that she was, she had heard gossip. "The bishop has not put you aside?" she faltered. She raised her crucifix. "He hasn't interfered with your work—with the building of the cathedral?"

The priest signified the worst. "My labor has been in vain," he acknowledged. "I am ordered from the parish like an incompetent. I thank God that she never knew!"

Sister Simplice shrank as from a blow. The suspended priest saw by the motion of her lips that she was praying. Her slender fingers clung fiercely to the rosary. She seemed to dread her own words. She could not trust her voice, dared not lift her face. Tears were slipping from beneath the delicate eyelids.

"Forgive me!" cried her confessor. "I dare not tamper with your faith. Forget that you have been listening I implore you."

The nun raised the dark fringes which had seemed a rebuke; but before she spoke, Father Barry was gone, vanishing behind the closed door of his mother's death chamber.

Chapter 9

Sister Simplice told her beads in vain. Strange new rebellion threatened her accepted life. Like the young priest in the room beyond, she doubted her right to wear the authorized habit of Roman Catholic faith. Tears scalded her cheeks; she could not keep them back. Yet to weep over an earthly tie long cut away must be counted a sin against her soul. The rosary slid from her grasp; then she caught it passionately to her lips. She had shed no tears for three whole years. Until to-day Sister Simplice had thought a victory won. Hospital work had seemed to bring relief to the woman unfitted for spiritual monotony. In the convent she had been misjudged. It was not until the mother superior comprehended the case, and removed her unhappy charge to an active field that things went well. Nursing the sick, the sister seemed to renounce the bridal veil which she had nearly worn. She regained courage, found joy in her patients. Actual service took unrest from her mind and heart. Gradually a romance interfering with devout prayers was put down. The nun went her way untouched by criticism. And it was doubtless intangible sympathy which had first made confidences easy between the sister and the priest. Their mutual struggle removed them from the spiritual line, when both tacitly owned that human longing abides in spite of prayer. But with the project of the cathedral absorbing the man, the gentle nun forgave her confessor and implored passionately for new strength for herself. In Father Barry the church had gained a splendid champion. Hospital work was a less brilliant opportunity; but at last Sister Simplice looked forward to passing years of peace. Until to-day she had been happy. Even yet she hardly understood the change which threatened her usefulness. She did not acknowledge that she had backslidden. Hysterical longing filled her woman's heart; she could not, would not analyze it. If she sinned she sinned! It seemed good to cry in view of impending penance.

The clock ticked away a full quarter while she sat in the hall alone with her thoughts. Then the door to the closed chamber opened and Father Barry passed out. He was pale, shaken. Instantly the nun became herself. Again she longed for service. "Will you not come below and eat something?" she asked. The priest shook his head.

"Not yet." He went on, but on second thought turned. "Tell Nora she must not offer me a hearty luncheon—I cannot eat it. She may bring toast and tea to my room. I must rest, be alone."

The nun's dismissal was plain. The sister went softly downstairs, hurt that she might not carry her confessor's tray.

Father Barry watched her glide beyond the landing, then walked quickly to his boyhood chamber. Here his mother had changed nothing. To retire at times to the little room was always like a snatched interview with himself. As a rule the dear lady had begged her son to use the more stately guest chamber, but to-day he shrank from the state apartment as one grown noted, yet now waiting for ignominy. To see his mother cold and lifeless had settled the half-considered step of the previous morning; for at last the man believed that he must give up the priesthood. He no longer wished to propitiate an archbishop. With his mother's death he was free. Had she lived, he might have gone on a hypocrite. Now all was changed. He need not continue a false life. Fortunately he was rich in his mother's right. He would not stay in the place which ought to despise him, and he might live in any part of the known world. At all events, he would emulate an honest citizen. He cast himself across the white counterpane of the bed and buried his face in the pillow. His neat, careful mother would never know that he had neglected to turn back the snowy spread. Outside, the dying blizzard moaned fitfully. Now and then a long, full gust came reinforced from distant plains; but the fury of the storm was over. He began to think of pressing matters. It was Tuesday. On Friday his precious mother must be buried. He sobbed aloud. Would the bishop stay official disgrace until after the funeral? Suddenly his only dread was public dishonor to his dead. As his mother's boy, he wept long and passionately. Nora's knock subdued outward emotion, while he took the tray from her hands. He saw that the faithful soul wanted to stop in the room, longed to fuss over her young master. But he gave no invitation and she went off grumbling. At the door she turned. "It's dyin you'll be yourself, ating no mate—only a bite of tasteless toast. And the bishop that old!" The parting shot brought no response. Nora closed the door with offended spirit. "He'll go under, with all the bother of his cathedral," she muttered. To live long enough to see her young priest a bishop was the old woman's earthly dream. She touched a crucifix in full view of the closed chamber where her mistress lay cold and still. Then she hastened below to clean and garnish. Sister Simplice had promised to stay until all was over, and she had also sent for Sister Agnes. Sister Agnes was cold and severe. The servant saw no need of two nuns. She went about the scrubbing and dusting, glad that she might work without regard to arriving cards or visitors. The good soul had prayed, then wept until she could hardly see. Now at last she was busy, again absorbed in material matters.

Meantime Father Barry forced down toast and tea. Details of his mother's funeral thronged his mind. She must have everything beautiful, all that a son could give. Her last Mass should be splendid; and again he wondered about the bishop. Would he officiate in spite of all? The widow's money would doubtless be remembered at a time like the present. Father Barry felt for a little blank book, and drew from his breast pocket Mrs. Doan's note and the enclosed check. Once more accident controlled his movements. Everything rushed back. Even in the midst of plans for his mother's Mass he thought of the letter he would write to Isabel. She must know the truth. Why had he not told her? Was he yet unable to confess himself a hypocrite to this woman whom he had once hoped to marry? After all, he could return her check by mail, for in writing he might explain an altered situation without demanding sympathy. But if sympathy came! If Isabel understood the case as it really was! Then she should help him to start over again, to go on with his life.

He worked himself into an exalted attitude. For the first time since the eventful interview with the bishop his self-esteem suggested a part removed from abject failure. As upon the ledge of the storm-beaten bluff, he felt once more a woman's governing presence. But the firm, commanding knock of Sister Agnes brought him from clouds to sinking sands. Again he was miserable—a false priest facing an austere nun, who would shrink away in horror as soon as she heard of his shame. The sister, supplanting gentle Simplice, held out a letter closed with the bishop's seal. Without waiting to read, the suspended priest knew the import of his superior's forced retraction; official action was rescinded until after his mother's funeral.

Chapter 10

Reginald Doan was out of danger. Infant tyranny and convalescence had both begun. Over clean-swept plains the blizzard of three days' duration moaned its last sharp protest. The sun blinked out through yellow grit on a city lashed white and ghostly. Isabel ran to her boy with the first peep of day. The little fellow still slept and she returned to a warm bed. The clock on her dressing table struck eight before she was summoned to the sickroom. The nurse opened the door, smiling. "He has been wishing for you. A night has done even more than the doctor expected."

"Has he been quiet?"

"Most of the time; but just before you came he was a wee bit naughty. Now he's going to be the best boy in the world."

Reginald stretched out his hands. "I wanted mother dear," he sweetly confessed. "I cried just one minute."

"But you must not cry at all," Isabel told him. "If you cry you may not get well enough to start for California."

The topic of travel was absorbing and soothing. Reginald lay quiet while his mother romanced of trains and engines and long dark tunnels. Genius for operating railroads had brought the boy's father to the top with several millions; the son would doubtless make good in the same way.

To-day Reginald clasped a toy locomotive in his baby hand. Interest in play was returning. "My ningin's all weddy for California," he exulted. "To-morrow I'm doing to div you a ticket."

"How kind," said his mother.

"And I'm doing to div Fadder Barry a ticket, too." Isabel made no reply. "I want Fadder Barry to come back—I want him so bad!" the boy petitioned. His accent seemed unduly broadened for the occasion. Long *a* fell like a wail.

"Don't be naughty," Isabel pleaded. "Father Barry cannot possibly come." Her voice broke, but she went on. "Listen and I will tell you why you must not ask for him. He has gone home—to his mother dear. Last night Father Barry's mother dear wished him to come to her, but he did not understand—he stayed with Reggie. Now Reggie is getting well." She rested a hand against her cheek to hide falling tears. "But I want Fadder Barry so bad!" the child protested. His baby face took on the resolute charm his mother dreaded. "I do want Fadder Barry!" he persisted. Then with autocratic movement he called the nurse. His countenance shone with expedient thought. "Teletone," he whispered, "teletone to Fadder Barry. Tell him to come back and bring his trunk." The attendant left the room, while the boy lay still and confident. His purple eyes shone so darkly in their wonderful sockets that the mother doubted the wisdom of an evident ruse. She waited anxiously until the nurse reappeared.

"Did you teletone?" the boy asked.

"I tried to," the woman answered, "but you see the wind has broken the wires. The poor telephone has a sore throat—just like Reggie; it cannot speak."

"Must the doctor make it well?" The child's sympathies were thoroughly aroused. For the first time the new nurse achieved a victory; and the illness of the telephone grew more alarming each moment.

The boy's mother went down to her breakfast, both hungry and happy. Reginald was in judicious hands. On a folded napkin was a letter, stamped for quick delivery. Isabel tore open the envelope and saw her returned check with sharpened senses. She began to read. When at last she understood, she was crying. "How unjust! How unjust to his ambition; to his struggle for accomplishment!" she choked. She tossed the check aside and re-read Father Barry's letter. His unhappiness was her own. Her one thought was to help him; to brace him against disappointment. This brilliant man—this friend—must not be ruined. There was some mistake. Those above him, the people who adored their priest, would see that he had fair treatment. Submission to a creed had not been part of Isabel's bringing up. Born and reared in an unorthodox atmosphere she had never been able to quite understand the power of Philip's church. It was, in fact, this very attitude which had first made trouble between them. The two had parted at Rome, both miserably conscious of their sacrifice, yet each blaming the other. Afterward, when the man became a priest, successful, eloquent, exerting splendid influence; appealing to people of all classes with his project for a cathedral that should mark an architectural epoch for the Middle West, the woman whom he had wished to marry—now residing in the same city—rejoiced that he had found a larger scope in life. When she suddenly became a widow she held it a pleasure to follow up the desirable friendship which was now strictly outside of sentiment. Father Barry's vestments covered the past. The two met without embarrassment. The priest was full of his cathedral; the young mother absorbed in her little son. Then when Mrs. Grace—a Catholic—confirmed at mature age and consequently over-zealous, arrived to live with her niece, Father Barry came more frequently to the stone house behind the elms. Soon he was the acknowledged friend of the family. Realizing that Mrs. Doan's interest in his new church was almost pagan, he still drew strange inspiration from her clear perception and balanced criticism. Without fear both man and woman accepted the cathedral as a bond which might prove to be more suitable than love. Isabel's actions were never confused with a flirtation. Thus far she had escaped censorious tongues. For Mrs. Doan was a personage in the western city and universally admired. But if she had escaped criticism, her aunt stood for a full share of it. The niece often despaired of her chaperone, regretting that she had selected one devoid of the finer feelings. However, she tried to make the best of an uncongenial arrangement which had resulted from blood relationship. And Mrs. Grace—a widow twice, and vaguely considering a third venture—was not altogether responsible for a light head and superficial education. She was generally adjudged amusing.

To-day Isabel was keenly sensible of great trouble. The priest's impending downfall, his heroic part in Reginald's recovery, the sudden death of his mother, were all sufficient reasons for her own straightforward determination. She would go to him—go to him at once—with no false shrinking. Perhaps even yet she might save him—induce him to appeal beyond his bishop. The weakness evinced in his letter, his wish to give up, to drift into obscurity—filled her with courage which she did not really understand. Yes, she must see him! talk with him, under his dead mother's roof—persuade him to hope; then she remembered that she was a prisoner in her own home, forbidden to leave it.

Chapter 11

Mrs. Grace stood dressed for the evening. She wore a rich black gown fitly relieved by transparent fillings. A splendid rosary of pearls and carnelians clung around her throat, while rare lace falling from the elbow drew attention to her plump arms and small white hands. Despite the woman's forty-seven years she was youthful in appearance. To-night she glanced into a full-length mirror, satisfied. As if loath to part from her reflection, she examined each detail of her elegant toilet.

"You are stunning," said Isabel, knocking lightly on the open door. "For myself, I thought it unnecessary to change my linen frock." As she spoke she threw back a coat of sable. "I thought I might go as I am, for I shall not enter the house. You have not been with Reginald, so of course there is not the slightest reason for not going in at a time like this. You can give Father Barry my lilies, and ask him to see me for a few moments outside."

"Simplicity becomes you," Mrs. Grace acknowledged. "You really look well without the slightest effort. I have always been improved by good clothes; even when I was a girl I shone in the latest styles. I do love up-to-date gowns." She ran a comb through her fluffy pompadour, which should have been silver but was counterfeit gold.

"Good gracious, Isabel, how your color has come back!" she enviously exclaimed. "When Reginald first took sick you were ghostly; now I believe you are fresher than ever. I can't understand you. Being shut away from everything has actually done you good!"

Mrs. Doan perceived the drift of her aunt's compliment. "You are certainly stunning in your new gown," she answered. "And you know I wish to get back to Reggie as soon as possible. Will you not come?"

The older woman moved slowly from the mirror. "About the flowers," Isabel went on; "only mine were sent—the lilies. The wreath you ordered will not be finished until to-morrow in time for service at the church. Grimes wrote me, explaining that the piece was so large that it could not be delivered sooner."

Mrs. Grace accepted a disappointment. "To-morrow will answer. I wish the wreath to be perfect." She followed her niece downstairs and outside to the waiting carriage. It was still cold, but the blizzard was dead in a shroud of stars. Mrs. Grace settled expansively, while Isabel protected her lilies as best she could.

"It is, after all, fortunate that my wreath was not sent," the aunt affirmed. "We never could have taken it inside, and Thomas might have objected to minding it on the box. When I asked you to telephone about it I did not realize how crammed a coupe is. The piece will be wonderful in the church—pink carnations, orchids, and maidenhair ferns. I am sure it will be the biggest thing of the kind Grimes has ever sent out. I preferred a cross, but so many were already ordered that I decided to have a wreath. I do hope Father Barry will like the color—pink suits his dear mother much better than white; don't you think so?"

Mrs. Grace judged grief by circumference and perpendicular measurement. It seemed as fitting to send her priest a wreath as large as a wagon wheel as it had been incumbent to wear the longest crape veil procurable during two distinct periods of widowhood. Isabel's armful of lilies struck her as shockingly unconventional, not even a ribbon confined the long green stems; and to Mrs. Grace this falling away from custom was highly amusing. But Isabel was Isabel. One never dared to count upon what she would do. Individuality was too strenuous for Mrs. Grace. Besides every one paid for good form, nowadays, while it was much easier to adopt accepted practice than to run the risk of appearing eccentric. Original people were generally poor—too "hard up" to be altogether proper.

"I should think you might have tied your flowers with white gauze and put them in a box," she said bluntly.

"Father Barry will like them as they are," Mrs. Doan answered.

The older woman sank back. A long feather on her large hat brushed Isabel's cheek. The niece moved away. In the corner of the carriage she held the lilies closer, praying that her companion might restrain frank opinions. Fortunately both women enjoyed independent fortunes. Affluence represented distinct value for each one. The aunt loved money for what it bought, the niece for what it brought. Mrs. Grace reveled in splendid things, Isabel in unusual opportunities. The one reverenced abundance, the other freedom and the luxury of not overdoing anything. Neither one was congenial with the other, yet for a time, at least, it seemed necessary for their conflicting tastes to remain politely sugared. Before the world aunt and niece appeared to be in well-bred harmony. To-night the irritating chatter of Mrs. Grace kept Isabel silent. Shrugged in her corner she scarcely heard, for suddenly she was wishing that she had written to her friend in trouble, instead of going to him. But for her aunt, she would have turned back. But Isabel had done many difficult things, things that other women shrank from. Her intuitions were fine, and she seldom regretted a first impulse. Almost at once Philip Barry's letter seemed rewritten for her eyes. Sentence by sentence she pondered the tempestuous, then broken, despondent appeal. Yes, he needed her; she was glad that she had ventured to come to him. A jar against the curb furnished Mrs. Grace with petulant opportunity, and while that lady settled her hat and adjusted her ermine, Isabel grew calm for an approaching ordeal. As her aunt alighted, hotly deploring the careless driving of a new coachman, a flood of light burst from Father Barry's temporary refuge. Two women, going forth from their dead friend's little home, tarried a moment with the son, who stood in the illuminated doorway. Suddenly the priest accompanied them forward. His eager eyes had clearly outlined a coupe and faultless horses. She had come! Isabel was before his house. He bade his neighbors a crisp good night and hurried to the side of Mrs. Grace. "So good of you, so good of you both!" he exclaimed, searching beyond for the lady's niece, still within the carriage. Mrs. Doan moved to the open door. "I was not intending to get out," she told him softly. "I came only with Aunt Julia, to bring these lilies for to-morrow, to let you know that I understand. When you have leisure to listen I want to help you to be brave and steadfast. You cannot—you must not give up." Her voice swept over him like music.

"Come in!" he commanded. "There is not the slightest danger for any one. My only visitors are Sister Agnes and Sister Simplice, both from the hospital."

Mrs. Grace, evidently annoyed, called from the footpath, "I am freezing!"

Isabel accepted the priest's hand, running forward. "Father Barry insists that I come in," she explained, while all three entered the house. Nuns, alert for notable callers, stood in the hall. Mrs. Grace shed outer ermine and clung significantly to her splendid rosary. In a room beyond she dropped upon her knees. The lady, addicted to posing, had unusual opportunity. The very atmosphere called for a graceful posture and devotional calm. In the presence of her recently bereaved confessor, flanked by praying nuns, she took no thought of Isabel standing apart an accepted heretic.

Mrs. Doan still wore her sable coat, the armful of blossoms resting like snow against the fur. She had stepped from darkness into light, unconscious of her dazzling appearance. Clasping the lilies, pressing them hard to still agitation, she might have been a saint of Catholic legend dispensing charity beneath flowers. "Come," said Father Barry, close at her side, "come across the hall." Isabel knew that he was leading the way to his beloved dead. She went softly, not wishing to disturb the kneeling aunt and devout sisters. Father Barry had spoken about his mother so often that at first she followed on as one entitled to a last privilege. At the threshold of an old-fashioned parlor she hesitated. "Come," the priest entreated. "She would be glad to know that you had placed the flowers with your own hands. Ascension lilies were her joy! she always chose them." Isabel moved slowly forward. The room, lighted with wax tapers, was long and narrow. At the extreme end stood the bier and improvised altar. There were beautiful flowers on all sides; the casket alone seemed to be waiting for the son's last offering.

"Will you not put them here?" He touched gently the spot of honor. "I should like to have them with my own, for I too have chosen lilies."

She thought of Reginald; of the difficult part in the boy's sick chamber which the priest had assumed, and thankfully complied. Father Barry watched her handle each lily with reverent touch. One by one she laid them down, then turned and smiled.

"How beautiful!"

"To me they are the symbolic flowers of the world," she answered.

"Yes," he told her, "they express my mother's life; it was white, pure, true, simple—fragrant with love." He sank his face touching the bed of bloom. "She lived perfectly," he went on in tender revery. "I never knew such faith—such faith in her friends, in her Church. And now I have lost her, lost her at the very time when she might have helped me. But thank God she did not know! Thank God always that she never dreamed the truth about her boy—about the priest she almost worshipped. And she could never have understood."

"I think she would have seen everything clearly, as you would have wished her to see it," Mrs. Doan protested. "I am sure she must have counseled you to be strong, begged you not to give up. She would have told you to wait—then to appeal your case to an authority higher than a very unreasonable old man. I do not understand your church government," she acknowledged. "I am too ignorant to advise you—yet surely there is some way, otherwise there would be need of neither archbishops nor of a pope!" She spoke valiantly. In her heretical judgment the Vatican had no significance if its ruler refused to step outside, to listen to individual cases of injustice.

"His Holiness bless your dear soul! bless you always!" the priest murmured huskily. His eyes glowed. "But you do not understand, do not see that it is not an ignominious downfall; not the bishop's power to keep me from going on with the cathedral, that has changed everything—made it impossible for me to remain a priest. All the time I have been nothing but a hypocrite, nothing but a coward."

"Do not say such things!" she cried.

"But I speak truth! Nothing shall ever silence my honest tongue again. You shall know at last why I went into a monastery, took false vows, adopted a sham profession."

She raised her face appealingly. Her whole being implored him not to hurt her again after the lapse of years.

"Forgive me!" he begged. "I am not blaming you, no one but my miserable self. I was not man enough to stand disappointment. The only way I could live! live without——" Isabel's eyes forbade him to finish. But he persisted. "The only way I could go on with life was to forget through forms, ceremonies, and flattery. When I began to work for the cathedral I had new hope. In reality I was less a priest than before. Yet I was more of a man, thank God! I intended to do my part like an honest architect. I wished to give my Church something worth while."

"And you will do so yet," she pleaded.

"Not now. I shall never act as priest again."

His words fell slow and hard. "I cannot live falsely one day longer."

The avowal deceived her; and now she had no fear for herself. Only the thought to help the man drove her on. Not being a Catholic, she was vaguely sure of the priest's words. For Isabel excommunication meant nothing but an unpleasant form which must eventually react on an intelligent victim. She held out her hand.

"Any one has the right to change. I am glad that you have decided so splendidly. It is like you to know when you have been wrong. And now that you have really found out you can begin all over—study architecture—build something as great as the cathedral. Vows that have ceased to be real are much better broken."

Her words evolved a simple plan. She had no understanding of the disgrace attending an apostate priest of the Catholic faith. Father Barry knew that she was innocent, that she had no wish to tempt him. But longing for all that he might still receive swept away his reason. He thought only as a man.

"And you will help me?"

"Why not?" she answered.

"Because you do not understand; do not know what your asking me to begin life over implies." His mother's face beneath the lid of the casket was no whiter than his own. All that he had lived through in the last three days made fresh renunciation vain. Discarded vows fell away from him as a cast-off garment. He was simply begging life from the woman he loved.

"Not here!" she pleaded. "Do not forget where we are!" Her voice broke. "You are still a priest; your vows hold before the world. I will not listen to you. Everything must be changed—absolutely changed, before I can see you—ever again." Her anger restored him.

"I will do anything!" he promised.

"Then go abroad—at once," she entreated. Voices admonished her to be prudent. She moved away. "I will help you! help you! But you shall wait. Nothing must shadow your honest life to come." She spoke in French, fearing her words might reach the hall. Mrs. Grace stood outside the parlor door. Dreading to look upon death, she yet resented her confessor's neglect. Nuns had ceased to hold her from an evident living attraction, as she swept into the room. But she was scarcely satisfied; for the length of the casket divided her niece from Father Barry. The priest, unconscious of an intruder, wept out his shame above Isabel's lilies.

Chapter 12

Isabel sat beneath the trees, while Reginald turned successful somersaults on the lawn. The boy was well and strong, adorable in blue overalls.

Mrs. Doan's second season in the most beautiful town in southern California had begun. She had forestalled the demand of tourists, and was already established in a furnished house, with a garden. She was very happy and believed that she had found the idyllic spot of a life-long dream. To-day a glorious perspective of purple mountains spread out before her, when she lifted her eyes from the bit of needlework which she was trying to finish for a friend's firstborn. Having spent the previous season in a large hotel she rejoiced in seclusion. Now she might face the future without indefinite dread, something she could not quite get rid of when thinking of the man whom she had undoubtedly influenced. For Philip Barry was no longer in orders. Almost a year lay between his life as a priest and the strained, difficult existence of one adrift, beginning over, feeling his way with a prejudiced public. But he had gone abroad, as Isabel advised; and at first excommunication appeared to be no harder to bear than his earlier Catholic punishment.

During months in Paris he had wrought himself into lofty independence, occupying his time with feverish writing. The result was an unpublished book on "The Spirit of the Cathedral." Disdaining many lurid accounts of his apostacy, he had worked with his whole intellect, thinking constantly of Isabel. Yet withal he kept his promise. Through six months he had sent her no word of his welfare. Isabel's pure name lent no color to a startling sensation, exciting the entire Middle West and Catholics throughout the world. With Mrs. Grace, alone, suspicion rested. For others, Mrs. Doan had no part in the priest's unusual course. Fortunately, but one stormy scene had ensued between the aunt and the niece, then both women agreed to ignore a painful subject. It was not until the second season in California, when European letters began to come with unguarded frequency, that Mrs. Grace again grew chilly. Glancing askance at foreign postmarks, she declined to ask the most trivial question concerning the man wholly excluded from the thoughts of a good Catholic. The lady's bitterness brewed fresh measure. Isabel was deeply hurt. Still, as during the previous winter, days passed without rupture. To all appearances things were as usual. It was not until Mrs. Grace rebelled over quiet that Isabel fully realized her aunt's unfitness. She now barely endured her chaperone, while more than ever she regretted the woman's unexecuted threat to return to apartments in a favorite hotel. However, Mrs. Grace stayed on, unsettling an otherwise contented household.

Isabel was obliged to keep open house without regard to chosen guests. A dream of freedom seemed ruthlessly dispelled. Yet to-day she was happy, at last free to indulge her thoughts. Early in the morning the restless relative had departed, and should good fortune continue, the touring car would not return before late afternoon. Isabel glanced down the gentle slope of her garden, shut in from streets beyond by hedge rows that in springtime were snowbanks of cherokee roses. Early rain had cleansed the mountains. The range was already prismatic, sharpened into fresh beauty below a sky as blue as June. No suggestion of winter touched the landscape. As usual the paradox for November was summer overhead and autumn on the foothills. "Old Baldy" still rose without his ermine. On the mesa brown and yellow vineyards lay despoiled of crops lately pressed into vintage or dried into raisins. What is known as "the season" had not begun. To Isabel the absence of the ubiquitous tourist, together with simple demands upon time, expressed a "psalm of life," which she might well have sung.

As she sat under a tree sewing, her mind went naturally to a land far distant—a land which held Philip Barry. For a letter had come that very morning. The excommunicated priest was in Paris awaiting her answer. A year of probation was almost over, yet he begged as a boy for shortened time. While Isabel worked she examined herself with judicial care. The unerring precision of each tiny, regular stitch seemed like testimony in her lover's case. She sewed exquisitely at infrequent intervals, and generally to compose her mind. Philip Barry's wish to come to her at once had upset both her plans and her judgment. Should she let him cross—two full months before the time agreed upon? All that her answer might involve pricked into soft cambric. She drew a thread, again and again struck back sharply into dainty space for a hemstitched tuck. It was hard—so hard—to refuse. Yet if he came, came within the month, then everything must be changed, not only for herself but for Reginald.

Isabel evaded the natural conclusion of the whole matter. As she sat below the towering mountains—very close they seemed to-day—she had a sense of being in retreat from everyone. She would take ample time to prove herself, to feel sure that her wish for Philip Barry's love was not selfishness. Nothing must make her forget the boy and the possible consequence of his mother's marriage to an apostate Catholic priest. She sighed, looking up at the purple peaks. The very serenity of her environment developed the longing for happiness. She was too young to accept blighting sacrifice. And yet, because of those two months on which she had counted, she was undecided. But withal she smiled. "He might have stayed away the year!" she murmured. Her son's glad shouts echoed on the lawn. Impatience is unreasonable. Why has he asked me to cable my answer? He should have waited for my letter, she told herself, in flat denial to what she really wished.

She sat idle. Stirring pepper boughs roused her from revery. She looked above at swaying branches, only to remember how admirably Reginald's father had waited for everything. Half stoical force, which described the man's power during a period of successful railroading, had always restrained him. When he died, his unsoiled record and splendid business success had both been achieved through the mastery of waiting. She smiled. The curve of her lips charmed. She was yet undecided. Yes, the man she married had not been impatient. He had waited three months for the one word she would not say. At last, when she became his wife, he still waited for something she could never give him. He did not complain. Again pepper branches trembled, and a shower of tiny berries began to fall. Commotion ensued among leaves, until a dark, slender mocker shot out, onto the back of Reginald's fox terrier. Suspicion, rage, shrieked in the bird's shrill war cry. The beleaguered dog retreated beneath Isabel's chair. The enemy flew off, but came back, finally to settle just below the cherished nest which his excitement had duly located. Egotism and pride made plain his secret.

Isabel laughed, as she patted the dog crouching at her feet. "Poor fellow!" she said. "You surely had no thought to harm domestic prospects." Then through the garden her boy rushed headlong, a toy spade swung recklessly, as Maggie the nurse pursued. Jewels of moisture glistened on the child's warm forehead. His cheeks glowed, the violet of his eyes shone flowerlike. He flung himself into waiting, outstretched arms. "O mudder dear!" he cried. "I just love you so, it most makes me cry." The joy of his baby passion, the depths reserved for years to come, seemed the expression of another, a stronger will; and Isabel knew that she had made ready her answer to Philip Barry.

Chapter 13

Shortly before five Isabel heard the horn of the returning car. She ran to a mirror and gazed at her reflection with new interest, for after useless struggle with Fate she had decided to let Philip Barry cross the water. The telegram had been sent to New York and soon her message would vibrate over the Atlantic cable. Early in the afternoon she had overhauled gowns not intended to be worn until several months later. Her changed toilet was a matter of significance, almost a challenge to her aunt, who would readily construe a transformation from half mourning to violet crepe and amethysts. She listened to the horn, dreading an ordeal. Fortunately, intuitions concerning Mrs. Grace always developed her own mastery. And to-day Isabel ignored the aunt's startled expression and crude outcry, as she hastened on to meet arriving guests.

"So glad to see you looking so well!" cried Gay Lewis, a school acquaintance of years back. "I was afraid we might be late! But luck is on our side, and with my mother, who so wishes to know you, are our very dear friends, Mrs. Hartley and her son." Miss Lewis assumed social responsibility with ease. While Mrs. Doan received the ladies, she fairly drove the man—or rather youth—of the party forward.

"Let me present you, Ned. And remember! I am doing something very sweet. Mrs. Doan is a darling to have us for tea; do you not think so?"

"You were kind to come," said Isabel, looking at young Hartley. "How did you manage to hit the hour exactly? Was there no trial of patience underneath your machine?"

"Not the least," Miss Lewis volunteered, as the strangers went onward to an immense living-room. "You should have joined us, not stayed at home on a day like this!"

Hartley's adoring eyes renewed a previous invitation. "You will come next time—to-morrow?" he implored.

"Have we not had a delicious run?" said Miss Lewis, speaking to the older women, relaxing in chairs and ready for tea.

"Yes, indeed," said her mother. "Everything has been perfect."

"And Mr. Hartley is such a precious driver," the daughter went on. "He left his chauffeur on the road—came home alone—without a mishap! You may fancy his skill from the time we made—ninety-nine miles, was it not? Yes, of course! a regular bargain run. And we started so late; not until after ten, with luncheon at one. Part of our way was simply drenched with fresh oil."

"Just like a greasy river," Mrs. Grace complained.

"An outrage upon strangers who wish to enjoy the country," chimed Mrs. Lewis.

"I should think people who live here—and many of them own most expensive cars—would protest. It doesn't seem fair to spoil good sport by such aggravating conditions," said Mrs. Hartley.

"Another biscuit, Ned dear; I am shamefully hungry." Gay Lewis, who had passed too many seasons of unavailable conquest to be accounted young by debutantes, leaned forward. "Dear Mrs. Hartley, take two. Such jolly biscuit, aren't they? Our hostess must indulge us all, we poor people who stop in a hotel."

She turned to Isabel, assiduously occupied with a steaming samovar. "You do it like an old hand; and I simply envy you this house." Miss Lewis swept the immense, rich room with alert eyes, keen to artistic values. "You were lucky. I am surprised that Mrs. Grant consented to rent. However, I am told that her stay abroad is apt to be protracted. You know she is most ambitious for her daughters?"

"Yes," assented Isabel, "she lives here only a few months each year."

"Is there a Mr. Grant?" asked Mrs. Hartley.

"Oh, dear yes; but he doesn't count. His wife has the money, and the taste, too," Miss Lewis volunteered.

"We must examine those antique brasses before we leave." Gay again addressed Mrs. Hartley. "Mrs. Grant has wonderful things," she explained.

"I always want to clean tarnished brass up a bit," the lady answered.

"Of course! I quite forgot your wonderful housekeeping."

Ned Hartley flushed at his mother's philistine candor.

"In this particular room, with its embrasures, dull richness, almost medieval simplicity, I should hardly dare to shine any landlady's cathedral candlesticks," said Mrs. Doan. The humor in her remark was not too plain.

"How charmingly the whole outside approaches into the very house," Miss Lewis put in. "There are no grounds in town quite so appealing. I love dear wild spots in a garden when vegetation admits of them. Where everything grows the year round it is a mistake to be too tidy with Nature."

"Mrs. Grant is an artist—a genius—in her way," the hostess rejoined. "She certainly understands semi-tropical opportunities, whereas some of her neighbors seem only to think of the well-kept lawns of an Eastern city."

"Since the town has grown so large and shockingly up to date, there is very little natural charm left anywhere," said Gay Lewis. "Really one has to have better gowns and more of them out here than in New York or Chicago. I never accepted so many invitations for inside affairs in my life before. I positively have no time for tennis, horseback, or golf. I just submit to the same things we do at home and spend almost every afternoon at bridge, under electric light."

Isabel laughed. "I am threatening to abjure electricity altogether in this particular room—burn only candles and temple lamps. I should like to try the effect of softened light on nerves," she confided. "After sitting in a jungle of the garden, I could come indoors and disregard everything but day-dreams."

"The test would be worth while," Gay agreed. "And really, I should like to have a day-dream myself."

"Absurd!" cried Mrs. Grace. "The room is dark enough already. With nothing but candles it would be worse than a Maeterlinck play. And how could one see cards by a temple lamp?"

"Won't you be seated?" Isabel asked of Ned Hartley, still standing. "You have worked so hard passing tea; do enjoy yourself." A momentous question went unanswered. "See! I am dropping preserved cherries into your cup—true Russian brewing. Delicious!" the hostess promised.

Hartley moved a chair. "May I sit here?" he begged.

"Of course. You deserve my fervent attention. Shall I give you orange marmalade with your biscuit?"

"Anything—everything!" he answered, all but dead to the sustained prattle of the other women. "It's awfully good of you to look out for me," he added, with an adoring glance. "And you will let me take you out in the machine—to-morrow?" he pleaded.

Isabel smiled. "You are very kind."

Miss Lewis was standing by the table with her cup. "We shall never let you rest until the thing is quite empty," she declared. "Cherries, please, instead of lemon. As I said before, you are a lucky, lucky girl to drop into such a place."

From a pillowed lair Mrs. Grace protested. "Don't tell her that," she begged. "The house and garden are well enough, to be sure; yet after all one comes from home to be free from care. I cannot understand Isabel's prejudice against hotels. There is nothing so pleasant as a good one, when one is a stranger in a strange land. I like life! something doing. Last winter we had bridge every afternoon and evening. The guests at the Archangel were delightful—so generous about buying prizes. And of mornings the Japanese auctions right down the street were so diverting. Of course we went every day—got such bargains, even marked Azon vases for almost nothing. It was so easy to buy your Christmas presents."

"How interesting," said Mrs. Hartley. "Do the auctions take place every season?"

"Always in the spring. And they are such an education!" Mrs. Grace persisted. "Then it is so exciting when you really want something. Of course one does not always know what to do with so many trifles, for often one does not expect to get caught on a bid. Still the sport is great and usually the things are good enough to send East to relatives, or else to give to maids about the hotel." Mrs. Grace laughed at her frank confession. "To be honest," she continued, "I am bored to death by our present mode of life. What Isabel finds in housekeeping I can't understand."

"Poor Aunt Julia!" Mrs. Doan flushed at an unexpected chance. "I see that I have been very selfish," she owned, mischievously. "Alas! I am too content to give up, after working hard to find so much! Then outside of personal delight—there is my boy. He is the happiest little soul imaginable! You should see him in his overalls! How could I deprive him of his home for another whole year?" the mother pleaded.

"He was well enough last winter," said Mrs. Grace.

"Dear Aunt Julia, our friends will think that we are quarreling. I had no idea that you were unhappy. As soon as the Archangel reopens you must take rooms and enjoy yourself as usual."

The woman, never prepared for a climax, rose from her pillows. "Take rooms at the Archangel! leave you unchaperoned!" she cried in blunt dismay. "Why, Isabel Doan, what are you thinking of?"

"I should not be alone," the niece answered. "My old French governess, Madame Sabot, is begging to come to California. By this time she is doubtless an ogress, well able to guard me."

A hot wave of suspicion swept the aunt's countenance.

"For that small matter," cried Miss Lewis, "I might do as well as madame. Take me for your chaperone! won't you, dear? I should love to act in the capacity. You know, a mere infant companion is all that is necessary nowadays—the best of form. And I am positively old, older than yourself," she coolly owned. Miss Lewis rose from her chair with vanishing hopes of Ned Hartley's continued devotion. The boy was heeding Isabel's slightest word.

"You must over think my application," she jested. "If Mrs. Grace decides to join mother at the Archangel I shall certainly hope to displace your French ogress. Meantime, we must be going. I have asked a man from the city to dinner; he will put in an appearance before I am fit. So sorry we cannot stop to see the boy in his nest. I understand he slumbers on a roof top—under the stars—like every one else out here. Isn't sleeping out of doors a fad? So admirable for the complexion! Really one might leave the country with a decent bank balance, if only one had nerve to rent an oak tree instead of rooms in a hotel." She chattered gaily above the others, to the verge of the waiting car.

While the machine gathered power, Ned Hartley hung on Isabel's promise just gained. "To-morrow—to-morrow at three," he impressed again. Miss Lewis heard his invitation, then blew the horn with ironic smile.

Chapter 14

Mrs. Grace had not accompanied the departing guests to the door. As the machine sped away Isabel realized her aunt's displeasure and braced against a scene. The time for plain words had arrived. She went slowly into the living-room, building up as best she could a line of defense for certain attack. By the glow of a wood fire, wreathing flame up the wide chimney, she saw her aunt's face; it was pale and tense with suspicion. Hate for the man, once her idolized confessor, had transformed the carefully preserved woman into one far from attractive. She seemed to gather vituperative force beyond her strength, for suddenly she stopped pacing the room to sink to a chair. Isabel turned, frightened.

"Aunt Julia! Aunt Julia, what is the matter?" She spoke, running forward.

Mrs. Grace motioned her away. "Don't pretend!" she cried. "I have seen from the very beginning—known exactly what you were both doing." Isabel said nothing. It was the older woman's opportunity. "Not building the cathedral was only an excuse for all that is still to come. You have ruined a man who otherwise must have been a saint!" She buried her face in her hands, which suddenly became gray and drawn beneath their weight of glistening gems. In anger, Mrs. Grace looked old.

"What kind of a life do you expect to lead with a traitor to both his faith and his honor? Do you suppose for a moment that he will forget! throw away his soul without longing to repent? I wish you joy of your conquest, Isabel Doan; and remember, I am telling you the truth, even though you have turned me from your house after all my devotion." Mrs. Grace sobbed hysterically. Isabel was at first stunned by her aunt's evil predictions; then she tried to speak. "You needn't excuse him!" the angry woman forbade. "I have heard your loose arguments before now. Don't tell me that it is better to break a sacred vow than to keep it with rebellion! I will not listen to you." She crossed herself against possible harm. "Read all the pagan books you can find; but don't forget my words. I must leave you as soon as possible, for, of course, after my treatment this afternoon I cannot intrude."

"Aunt Julia!" Isabel sank at her feet. "Please let us part friends," she pleaded. "You have been very good to me; if only you could understand—let me tell you things which you do not know——"

Mrs. Grace sprang up.

"And you intend to really marry that man!" Isabel flamed scarlet. "You actually expect to go through with the farce of a religious service? Well, you had better remember that marriage vows are more easily broken than any others. Don't be a fool—a prude about mere form—if you care to keep a lover; for mark my words, the man who has been untrue to his Church will find it much easier to forget a wife." Vindictive zeal gave Mrs. Grace hard fluency. And the insult which Isabel had not expected made her own part clear. She rose from the floor straight and firm.

"I feel that it is not too late for you to leave me this evening; if you think differently, I can take Reginald and Maggie into Los Angeles while you find another home. After what you have said it is impossible for us to sleep beneath the same roof."

Her wounded womanhood stood out superbly. She walked from the room. Above, with her door locked against every one, she burst into tears. With burning face in the pillow she wept out her heart. In all her life she had never felt so hurt and miserable. Would the world regard her marriage to Philip Barry in the same wretched light as her aunt? Then perhaps the Catholic woman was right; after all she—a heretic—might not be able to hold the man who was now willing to give up everything for love. And she had induced him to take the fatal step. Perhaps she did not understand the force of Catholic vows.

She sat up, gazing through the window at the full top of a eucalyptus tree, dark, and wonderfully etched against lingering gold of sunset. Why should she be miserable in a world as lovely as the one about her? She longed for the happiness which belonged to her youth and station. Again she recalled every word which she had said to Philip Barry at the side of his mother's casket. To her straightforward nature she had advised him wisely. With reason unbiased by dogmatic training; with her soul, honest as a child's, she felt no shame for what she had done. And it was now too late to hesitate. She had sent the message and she must hold to it with her life, her womanhood. She bathed her eyes, still going over the main facts of her lover's disgrace in the Catholic world. She came back always to the main point; he only committed a mistake when he had gone into the priesthood without realizing the price. He had tried in vain to live a life of self-denial, of enforced conformity, whereas both attempts were totally unsuited to his temperament and mentality. He had made a false step in the wrong direction; why, then, should he go on? It were better to stop than to stumble and fall. When a lawyer failed in the profession none thought worse of him when he succeeded with literature. And the doctor, unable to grasp physical ills of casual patients, carried no stain on his honor if he discovered some other calling. It could not be right to denounce a physician in charge of souls because he would not go on with a spiritual travesty. Philip's disappointment in regard to the cathedral, his unjust treatment by his bishop, his thwarted ambition,—these things she put to one side in a final summing up. All seemed secondary to the confession of the man who had stood by the side of his dead Catholic mother. He had said that he could no longer continue his priesthood, because he had ceased to be false with himself. That to Isabel made sufficient reason for all that had happened—for all to follow. She covered the case by direct standards of her own truthful nature. This evening, looking into the golden sunset, she could find no justifiable bar to marriage with Philip Barry.

When Maggie tapped on the door she opened it calmly. The girl was vaguely conscious of sudden disturbance. "Come in," said Mrs. Doan. "Mrs. Grace is leaving this evening," she explained. "If possible, you must help with her packing. I shall not be down to dinner. I am tired and will lie down outside with Reginald; you need not disturb me. Should I need you I can ring." Isabel had partly undressed.

"You won't have anything to eat?" the nursemaid questioned.

"Nothing now, perhaps later." Mrs. Doan hastened to put on a padded robe. Her hair fell about her shoulders.

She separated the shining mass, weaving it into braids, as she went, almost running, to her sleeping son. An upper balcony, partially protected by canvas, made his cozy nest. At the south and east there was nothing to shut out the stars, while at dawn peaks beyond the northern range rose dark and sharp through zones of burning rose. Isabel cast herself upon her own bed. Delicious air cooled her burning cheeks and she could hear the gentle, regular breathing of her boy. She had no thought of sleep. Her only wish was to escape to a place cut off from her aunt's temporary territory. Now she would wait. Her heart was kind, and in retreat she began to feel sorry for the woman with whom she had parted. Mrs. Grace was only half sister to Isabel's father, and far back the little girl had wondered why her pretty aunty so often quarreled with her family. Once she heard her father declare that Julia's nose and hands seemed to guarantee a lady, but she had caught no more. At the time she did not understand; since then she had grown older and wiser. She sank upon the pillow gratefully. Below there was a stir of running feet, a commotion at the telephone. Isabel tried to forget her own inhospitable part. Once she half rose from bed, half believed that she would face her hysterical aunt with overtures of peace. Then she felt the foolishness of going through with everything again. Mrs. Grace was impossible after what had taken place. Sounds about the house continued. The angry woman proposed to take her own time for packing; and it was nearly midnight before Isabel became sure that an unwelcome guest had gone. Above with the boy, she watched the stars grow brighter, listened to night calls of stirring birds, wondered about Philip Barry at the other side of the world. Now at last she was alone in the house with Reginald and the servants. She got up and went below, to find Maggie crying in the hall. The girl hid a crimson face and Isabel knew that Mrs. Grace had enlightened her in regard to a coming event. As one Catholic to another, she had warned the nursemaid to protect her soul from evil influence.

"You may go to bed," Mrs. Doan commanded. Maggie turned away, then came back. Her voice failed and she pointed to the dining room, where a little supper was daintily set out. She sobbed her way to the back of the house, then above to her room. Isabel was alone. She had hardly dreamed of freedom, yet now it was here. The fire in the living-room still burned; and like a child, she took a bowl of milk and bread and sat down on a rug before glowing embers. In spite of all she felt happy. She was hungry, too; and after she had eaten every mouthful she sat on,—thinking of Philip.

Chapter 15

It took Isabel nearly a month to throw off the effect of her aunt's angry departure. At the end of that time the cheery French woman arrived to take the place of Mrs. Grace, who had gone from the town to St. Barnabas. Still later, Isabel heard with strange relief that her aunt no longer enjoyed California and was about to seek excitement in New York. She felt glad that Mrs. Grace would be at the far side of the continent before the coming of Philip Barry.

Isabel had not kept her engagement with Ned Hartley the morning after the trouble; but the next day and for days following she toured in the machine with the elate boy and his mother. Mrs. Lewis and Gay were often of the party. To spin through a country growing fresher, more enchanting with each welcome rain was a tonic. Isabel rebounded. And at last Philip had started for home. She now thought of little else and her heart grew light as days slipped away. To restore the man whom she had unduly influenced; to bring him in touch with happiness; to lead him in his new career to honor, even to fame, grew into a passionate hope as time went by. Philip was already hers. She would make him forget, help him to consecrate his talents anew to art and letters. He must write books and be glad that he was no longer a priest, bound with forms and obsolescent vows. His brilliant mind should be free to develop, his manhood to grow unrestrained. Isabel's own unorthodox view was so wholly conceived out of intellect and evolving mercy that retribution and remorse were not pictured as possible punishments reserved for an apostate Catholic once a priest.

Her one thought was to make the man who had suffered from an almost fatal mistake happy. When once he felt the surging joy of love, opportunity, his past life would cease to trouble him. Isabel was young and confident. She felt sure of everything. The day, wonderfully bright and exhilarating, called her into the garden, where she found Reginald. The boy had dug a flower bed with a tiny spade; then, too impatient to think of seeds, had broken full blooming geraniums into stubby shoots and planted each one with a shout of laughter.

"See my garden! mother dear," he cried, as Isabel approached. "It's all weddy—growed beau-ti-ful!" He clapped dirt-stained hands and bounced about in his blue overalls.

Maggie raised a tear-stained face from where she was sitting. Her only outlet seemed to be weeping. "To think that I must leave him!" she sobbed. "It breaks my heart to go, and nothing but Mike insisting that we get married could part me from my boy." She wound her arms about her little charge. Mrs. Doan saw that the girl held a letter. "It's to San Francisco he bids me come," she went on. In her excitement she had lapsed into old-country expression. "And he thinks I can get married with no warnin'. Married indeed! Married without a stitch but store clothes. I would like to send him walkin' back East, with the chance of a better man."

"You must not do that," said Mrs. Doan, now reconciled to the girl's departure. Reginald was growing fast, and with Madame Sabot and an English nurse in readiness to fill the Irish maid's place, the boy would find his daily education an easy matter.

"Poor Maggie's so sick, mother dear," the little fellow explained. He threw his arms about the neck of his weeping nurse, kissing her loudly. "Now poor Maggie is all well!" he exulted. "Didn't Reggie give Maggie a nice, big, fat kiss!" He went back satisfied to his miniature garden, while at the same moment Ned Hartley rushed down the terrace. "Where are you all?" he cried. His manner had grown free and confident since his first tea-drinking in Mrs. Doan's drawing-room. This morning his boyish face glowed with expectation. "Do hurry," he begged. "You are surely coming? 'The mater' is waiting in the machine and the day's bully." He pressed his wish at Isabel's side. She led him beyond the range of Maggie's ears.

"I am afraid that I cannot go; Reginald's nurse is leaving at once," she explained.

"But I have found your horses!" young Hartley tempted. "You must come and pass judgment on the finest span in the country. They are beauties—perfect beauties! I ran the owner down by mere chance; and we'll find him on a foothill ranch, with the pair in question, saddle horses, too. You simply must come if you really wish for a snap." His enthusiasm was contagious.

"You are good," Isabel answered.

"Then you should reward me with your company. Bring old madame and the boy."

Reginald's ears had caught the invitation. "Come, mother dear!" he cried. "Come wight away." His glee bubbled. The uncomprehended tears of his nurse were forgotten as he placed his hand in Ned's.

"See the mischief you have wrought," said Isabel. "It is too late for Reggie to go from home—almost time for his bath and nap," she announced decidedly.

"But, mother dear," the blue eyes flashed mutiny, "But, mother dear, Reggie *must* have a good time!" The ruling passion of the age possessed the infant's soul; to enjoy life topped every other thought.

The child drew Hartley forward with all his strength. "Come right away," he coaxed. "I want to get my red coat."

"But darling," Isabel protested, "you cannot go in the machine this morning. Here comes Maggie to give you your bath; go with her at once."

A struggle was on. "You must go with nurse. You may not have a good time this morning. Another day you shall ride in the automobile if you are obedient."

The child surveyed his mother. She showed no sign of weakening. For an instant his lips trembled; a cry half escaped them, then he rushed into Maggie's arms.

"To-morrow Reggie may go, to-morrow!" he repeated with baby confidence. Two sturdy, adorable legs went peaceably forward across the lawn. With every step the boy evoked some happy future day—a glad to-morrow.

"You're the slickest mater on record!" exclaimed Hartley. "How do you do it? I believe you might subdue a labor strike if you tried. No man could resist you long. And any fellow would be bound to do things, make something of himself, if only he might have you to keep him level." That he had known Mrs. Doan but a short time escaped his mind. Suddenly he was pushing his cause with youthful ardor. "If you could only care for me!" he cried. "Only believe that I really would amount to something if you gave me the chance. Why can't I prove it to you? Indeed, I would do everything that you wished me to—be as good as Reg—upon my word!" Isabel raised startled eyes in mute entreaty. "Let me finish," the boy implored. "I know just what you think, so please do not tell me. You have heard about the scrape at college, all about my getting fired, my father's anger, everything abominable. And it is true, all true,—I was an ass, a perfect ass. I admit it. But you see I'm different now. I can be a man, even if I didn't get through college by the skin of my teeth. If you would only marry me father would overlook everything! set me up in any kind of business I liked. And besides, 'the mater' has much more money than dad. She's simply crazy about you—almost as crazy as I am."

"My dear boy," cried Isabel, feeling very wise and old, "you must stop. If you say another foolish word our pleasant friendship will have to end right here."

"But it isn't foolish to love you, to be mad with good resolutions for your sake," he pleaded. "Of course, if you won't listen to me now I must wait. And I will wait—wait just like Reg—until to-morrow!" His whole being reflected new resolve.

"Then be reasonable. Go back to college; finish the course your position in life demands; please your father; be good." They moved slowly to the house.

"And I may hope when I get my sheepskin?"

"No! no!" she cried. "I meant nothing of the kind. I could never, never marry you. Even if——" she hesitated—"it can never be," she finished.

"Then there is some one else?"

"There is some one else," she answered in a voice so true that its cadence hurt the more.

Ned looked upon the ground; then he lifted hopeless eyes. "Of course I am an ass; I always was one. But you will come out in the machine? I haven't the nerve to explain; and I'll help you find the horses—for the other man——" he choked out.

Isabel could not refuse the humble request.

Chapter 16

The luxurious touring car sped away. In the tonneau Mrs. Hartley and madame chatted with no suspicion of Ned's unhappy state. The morning was glorious.

"Please come," the boy had begged; then added, "if you don't, 'the mater' will want to know the reason why."

"We must be the best of friends," Isabel whispered, as she took her place in front.

"Is ze country not de-vine?" cried the old French woman. "So like La Riviera! my southern France!"

Mrs. Hartley coughed. "The dust is a drawback," she complained.

"But it does not rise in ze nostril—drive upon ze face; there is no wind to make rough ze flesh," the other argued. "At San Francisco ze little stone rise from ze ground, hit ze eye! And in Chicago ze wind blow fierce, make sore ze throat." Mrs. Hartley tightened her veil. "Ze south California is good—dear Madame Hartley—good beyond every land but France." Madame Sabot laughed like a happy child. "Am I not blessed to stay in ze paradise? To live wis my angel children? Since ten years I have no home—only trouble. Tes grande!" she cried, "ze tree; I forget ze name."

"Eucalyptus," prompted Isabel, turning backward.

"U-ca-lip-tus," madame repeated. "Not trim like ze Lombardy poplar, but so tall! so tall!"

The giant stood by the wayside. The round, smooth trunk, expanding each year from beneath girders of loosening bark, lifted a weight of inaccessible white blossoms to the sky. Peeled to a shining mauve, the mighty stalk shot up to swaying, dull green branches. From lower irregular limbs long ribbons of sloughing fiber hung in the gentle breeze, until rain or a transient gust sent them rattling to the ground. When threatening moisture lay along the range the giant eucalyptus loved to plunge into inky clouds, to bend anon, a towering helmet of sable plumes. This every artist saw; and in her own excitable way the French woman felt the passion of the wayside monarch.

"Tres grande!" she cried, with parting wave of her hand.

"I see no beauty in a eucalyptus," said Mrs. Hartley. "If I had a place here I should not have one of them about—such untidy trees! It would drive me distracted to see loose strings swinging overhead. Then when the fiber drops it is even more annoying. Falling leaves are bad enough, but falling bark! I could never endure that. At Lakeside—our country place—Mr. Hartley and Ned rave over dried maple leaves; but I assure you I have them raked up each morning. I really could not endure the autumn if I permitted myself to be buried under dead leaves. I should be too blue. With rheumatic gout I am miserable enough."

"But ze California will make ze cure. Not one bad head since I find ze happy land," old madame declared.

The chatter at the back of the car made rare entertainment for Isabel, who listened by reason of Ned Hartley's unsociable mood. The boy was deep in sulks. He ran the machine so carelessly that his mother began to complain.

"Don't be cross; please be nice," Mrs. Doan begged, softly.

They were skirting the foothills, headed for an upland ranch.

"Won't you prepare me a little for what I am to see—tell me about the horses?" she coaxed.

"There isn't much to tell," Ned answered, out of gloom. "I just happened to notice the span in town; then I traced their owner through a livery stable groom. You may not like them," he added, with trying unconcern.

"I am sure that I shall love them. And it was good of you to go to so much trouble." The boy's rudeness should be ignored. "Did you know that I have always been wild about horses?" He made no response and she went on. "Ever since I was a small girl I have loved to gallop over the country. Now I am going to indulge myself; have not only a carriage span, but two saddle horses—the very best ones we can find."

"I presume Reginald is about to mount?" Ned was madly jealous. The question brought a flush to Isabel's cheeks.

"I expect him to ride," she answered, "but of course on a pony."

The automobile landed in a rut, then bounded upward and onward. "Why, Ned!" cried Mrs. Hartley. "What is the matter? If you can't run the machine more evenly you had better bring Adolph when next we come out." The rebuke was smothered in a rhapsody by madame. "Behold!" she cried, "behold ze landscape!" But the too evident attempt to allay the mother's criticism fell flat. The lady continued to suffer with every jar. Neither the dazzling contour of the lifting range, nor a wonderful valley, sweeping from foothills to the distant, glistening sea, could distract her mind from personal complaints.

It was a relief when a sudden detour landed the machine on a cross way, leading through interlacing pepper trees, to a small but attractive bungalow. A pretty, neatly dressed young woman sat on the porch sewing. She rose as the car stopped.

"Good morning," she said, "my husband is with the horses." She pointed to whitewashed paddocks at the left some distance beyond the peppers. "Please keep going, the road leads straight; my husband will hear the machine."

"Thank you," said Mrs. Doan. "You are fortunate to have such a location for your home. You must enjoy living here?"

"Oh, we do. Of course not every one cares for a foothill ranch, but we are never lonely." She had a flowerlike face and her simple refinement was charming. "I hope you will like the horses," she went on. "Now that we have decided to let two of them go, the quicker the better." She laughed musically, then explained. "My husband has often refused to part with his famous four, since they won the chariot race, two years ago. You have heard about New Year's Day in Pasadena? All strangers look forward to the flower parade, followed by genuine Roman chariot races. And the running of thoroughbreds, four abreast, is fine!" Her blue eyes kindled.

"I should think your husband would try again," said Ned.

"Oh, he will, but with a different four. He does not wish to repeat his victory with the same horses, for last year there was trouble."

"Possibly he might part with the noted quartette? If two of them answered for the saddle—are not too wild," Mrs. Doan added.

"Oh, no," the young wife answered. "Hawley would never consider selling Delia or her running mate. We could not let those two go." She flushed with her ingenuous confidence. "Delia is named for me. A little romance in which she took leading part must always insure her pasture on our ranch."

"Come with us in the machine," said Mrs. Hartley. "Do be good enough to show us 'Delia,'" said Mrs. Doan. "We are now doubly interested in your husband's horses."

Isabel smiled in her rare way. The woman of the foothills had once been a school teacher and felt the irresistible charm of the beautiful stranger's manner. To peer at life below the mesa was an opportunity, and the rancher's young wife threw aside a fresh gingham apron and entered the car. She sat in the center, half turned in a revolving chair, where her eyes covertly caught the elegant but simple effect of Mrs. Doan's morning toilet. She had never seen any one so neatly put up against ravages of wind and dust. Isabel's earlier freshness remained;

and the large purple hat securely veiled for touring seemed duly created to protect her golden hair. The older ladies were kind and the little woman of the foothills enjoyed the short spin through the avenue of peppers to paddocks beyond.

"You never lock your door?" Mrs. Hartley questioned.

"No, indeed. No one would think of stealing up here! Every one is honest where every one sleeps, eats, and lives out of doors."

"Of course," said Isabel. "How wonderful this upland country is; I envy you a home beneath the mountains. How close they are!" She swept the range in contemplative joy; then her eyes dropped to paddocks, outlined by whitewashed fences, but naturally adorned within with huge live oaks. The spreading trees made shelter for all seasons. "Happy horses!" she exclaimed. "I am not surprised they won the chariot races."

The rancher's wife looked pleased. "My husband is very proud of his stock," she answered; "and here he is."

Cole met them, tall and sun browned.

Without further pleasantry the party plunged into business. The little woman who had brought the strangers thither realized an impending sacrifice. To part from any one of a noted "four" was hardly to be borne. Then she remembered that Hawley needed money; that lithe, slender "Delia" and her running mate were not to be sold. When a purchase price became definite she smiled, although she felt like crying. The trade assumed reality; and Ned Hartley, emerging from sulks, became interested. But his good nature did not last, for soon he understood that Isabel Doan was about to buy thoroughbred horses for the enjoyment of another man. The boy was mad with jealousy. He was sorry that he had urged the trip to the foothills. Then all at once he felt superior, very like a martyr, in view of all that he suffered and proposed to suffer for years to come. Meantime Cole put his horses through telling paces. No points of the beautiful pair were overlooked. Mrs. Doan acknowledged her wish to close the bargain, but the rancher evinced no haste. Finally it was agreed that the span should go to town for a week. A friend of Cole's would take care of them, while Mrs. Doan might drive each day, with the privilege of returning them. In case the trade went through, a permanent coachman and a groom would be duly recommended. Isabel's appointments from her own stable had recently arrived and now she could hardly wait to try the thoroughbreds in different styles of vehicles.

"I shall accept your kind offer," she declared, smiling. "And you will remember the saddle horses? I wish for two beauties, as soon as possible."

She was radiant, thinking first of Philip, of all that she was making ready for his new life—a life which must be perfect. "Automobiles shall never make me give up the joy of owning horses!" she declared.

Ned Hartley bit his lip and turned away. Down in the valley he saw emerald growth flashing in sunshine. Spreading acres of orange orchard, trees always dressed in green swept onward from cleansed mountains and reviving foothills, to a distant line of blue—the ocean. The landscape was glorious, but the boy felt bitter and would not regard it. He joined the rancher's wife with pretext of renewed interest in her favorite. Mrs. Cole was feeding "Delia" sugar as Hartley approached. "We call her our baby," she explained. "I never dare meet her without offering sugar; I always carry a few lumps with me." To-day the high-spirited animal stood eating from the hand of her mistress, so gentle that Ned could hardly reconcile her present range with that of the track.

"Will she run in the chariot races the first of January?" he asked, not caring, yet wishing to appear at ease.

Mrs. Cole shook her dark head. "I think not," she answered. "My husband hardly expects to drive this year. Next season, with two young horses trained for running with Delia and her mate, he will try again. Last New Year's there was a great deal of trouble about prize money, in spite of the evident dishonorable driving of a certain man who fouled my husband's chariot. Oh, but it was exciting!"

Ned begged for the story. The rancher's wife went on.

"Hawley had virtually won the race; had taken the pole from his opponent on the first dash, just beyond the judge's stand; he was holding his advantage without difficulty, when beyond the second turn his right wheel was deliberately knocked off. Of course the big race of the day was ruined. The management of the tournament has done everything to induce Hawley to run his four this season, but he has refused." Her cheeks flushed with the thought of her husband's humiliation.

"Will the man who fouled the chariot be permitted to drive again?" Hartley asked, with interest in foothill scandal.

Mrs. Cole looked proudly away to the sun-browned man approaching. "Please do not speak of last year's race," she pleaded. "I dare not let Hawley know how I distrust the neighbor who fouled his chariot. But of course nothing was proved. It was but the word of one man against another, for the trouble took place too far from the judges' stand to be exactly defined. With some it passed as an accident. Then you know it was all so quick—the thundering by of the chariots—the crash!" She clasped her hands as Cole came nearer, then smiled at Mrs. Doan, who seemed a vision of happiness.

Terms had been agreed upon and the horses were to be taken to town at once. But Mrs. Hartley had grown impatient. Not wishing to make the lady late for luncheon, Isabel brought her own affair to an abrupt close. "I am sure to keep them! I love the beautiful creatures already," she declared, as the machine shot away.

The little woman of the foothills did not return in the car.

"If the horses must go I am glad that she is to own them!" she cried, when her husband named the price. "Do you suppose she will marry the young man?"

Cole shook his head doubtfully. "Can't say for sure; but if sulks are any indication, should say the boy was down on his luck. I think there must be another one; and by George! he ought to be president, or at least a senator, to splice with such a woman."

"I'm not a bit jealous," his wife answered. "I think just as you do. I think she's the most gracious being I ever met."

"She's a prize package, all right," Cole said. "And she has a mind of her own. The way she settled on the horses in less than twenty minutes shows that she's used to money. Most women would have taken three weeks to decide, coming back to haggle at least a dozen times." He cast his arm around his wife's trim waist, urging her gently down the road. "I'm as hungry as a wolf," he confessed. "Let's get something to eat; then we'll drive the span to Pasadena and price pianos. We'll have a corker! One that plays itself."

She cried out joyously. After all, she might have something, too, like the favored woman who could look, then choose at will. Isabel spinning away from the foothills was still happy with thoughts of the morning's transaction. Very soon her stable would be ready for use. The span, saddle horses, a pony for Reginald were all in her mind. And she must have a touring car and an electric runabout besides. The house was already equipped with servants, including a first-class celestial cook, who achieved culinary mysteries with smiles and good nature. Madame had arrived to stay, and when the English nurse displaced Maggie life might move along with the spirit of Arcady. Then he would come! Philip, her once forbidden lover.

Chapter 17

Weeks later washouts on the desert demoralized all overland trains, and Isabel waited impatiently for the belated "Limited." Then at seven in the evening she heard Philip Barry's voice over the telephone. In an hour he promised to be with her. During the morning she had wandered about the garden, trying in vain to picture the meeting with the man whom she had not seen for nearly a year. By afternoon she was in a fever of suspense. Throughout the house she had arranged flowers, with her own hands had cut great bunches of roses for the living-room. A few candles were already lighted, while blazing logs made home-like cheer. Isabel stood before the fire, waiting. She could not sit on a chair, with the clock in the hall ticking away loud seconds. To-night she wore soft white, with pearls. Her lover would be pleased to see her out of black. She wished his first moment to be full of joy.

"Ma belle angele!" madame cried again and again. French ecstacy continued until Isabel begged for no more compliments. She kissed the old brown cheeks, then with sudden impulse fled above to her sleeping boy. Reaction had come at the end of a long, long day. The felicitous moment she had fancied was suddenly uncertain. Something she dared not define frightened her. All at once Reginald's soft breathing seemed reproachful.

"Dear little son," she whispered, "mother loves you none the less, and he—will love you, too." She put her bare arm about the boy's warm body and kissed his cheek. Tears came into her eyes. She hardly knew whether she felt glad or sad. "Good night, little son; Father Barry is coming—'Father Barry,' who loves us both." Something told her to hope; and the clock in the hall was striking eight. All that had happened—all which was yet to happen—seemed like a dream. She had waited so anxiously, heard so often through the long day far-away trains whistling through the valley. To-night she scarce believed her summons when it came. But the maid had opened the outside door, and Isabel heard it shut. A man's voice spoke her name; Philip Barry was below. At the landing of the staircase she reached weakly for a card, dropped it, then went slowly down.

Philip waiting in the bright, rich room saw her coming. He stood unconscious of his lately changed appearance, his evening clothes. A London tailor had assured him that he was now properly dressed for the way of the world, and at last his "priest's garb" was forgotten. His worshipful face, slightly thin, expressed only joy as he ran forward. But something was wrong with Isabel. Something seemed to be lost from the lover imploring at her side; and she shrank, holding him aloof for judgment.

"What is it?" he cried. "Am I not welcome?" He scanned her face with passionate longing. "Do you regret—regret letting me come?"

"No, no," she faltered. "Only wait! wait until I get used to you."

He took her at her word and moved away. Hunger tried his soul. But he made a braver lover than he had been a priest.

"What did you expect?" he asked at last.

"Father Barry!" She was crying.

He gathered her close.

"Be patient," she begged. "The train was so late—so long, long coming—and—and you see I must get used to your vest not being fastened in the back."

He smiled pitifully. "Will you ever forget? Ever be able to go beyond those mistaken years? Can you not go back to the time when we first knew each other?"

"Yes, we will both go back. I will forget! I promise you. But tell me—" she was dazzling in her excitement—"tell me if you are sure! Have you never been sorry for what I made you do? You might have gone on, might have overcome things which seemed beyond your power. It was because I came that night in the midst of your trouble, when you were not strong enough to drive me from you. If I had stayed away?" She put the situation plainly, waiting for his answer as a soul on trial. She was jealous now, even of a possible, passing regret. "If I had stayed away?" she repeated.

"I should have left the priesthood," he told her simply. "I had found out—knew certainly that I could not go on, even before I saw you. Your coming to me when my mother went but gave me hope, brought rescue. Before God I am now honest!"

She threw her arms about his neck. All that she had withheld was waiting. Love blazed in her starry eyes, on her wonderful lips. Every doubt had gone with Philip's last words. Everything seemed clear—straightened out. Hours sped as moments. There was so much to talk about, so much to explain away. Each one went back to the beginning and to a time forbidden even in memory to an honorable wife, to a priest. Intermediate existence was soon wiped out. Then Isabel thought of her boy, now Philip's boy as well. They would bring the child up jointly. She was glad, very glad. "And you will love him always?" she implored. "He has not forgotten you; kisses your picture every day. You shall help me with his education. I am so anxious not to make mistakes. You know Reggie's warm, live temperament? You will advise me?"

"I was not wise about my own career, but I will do my best for the boy," Philip humbly promised.

Isabel saw for the first time how much he had suffered. He looked older, haggard, despite his happiness. But his face had assumed grave sweetness. The old assurance of a once popular priest was gone. Dependence upon love would give him courage to begin over. The fullness of Isabel's rich nature swept outward to his need. "We shall be happy, I feel it, I feel it!" she whispered joyously.

Chapter 18

Isabel awoke, fully conscious of the day just dawning. From her bed in the half-open sleeping porch she peered into a roseate east. With her whole heart she went out to meet the sun, slowly lifting from a rampart of dark mountains. This was Isabel's wedding day. At high noon she was to be married to Philip Barry. She rested on her elbow, waiting for the transcendent moment. She was a "sun worshiper" for the time, and not a cloud subdued the oncoming spectacle. As Isabel watched, the sable range took on softest blue, while snow-crowned peaks rose dazzling in the distance. Over the world the sun poured light. And this was her wedding day. It was still too early for a bath, too soon to begin her simple bridal toilet, and she fell back on the pillow. The white broadcloth gown and coat with feather-trimmed hat were ready, and the night before Philip had brought a bouquet of dewy-eyed forget-me-nots. She had chosen the flowers in preference to all others. There was very little to do, no more than for an afternoon call. She smiled over enjoined simplicity, glad that neither bridesmaids nor guests should claim thoughts which might all belong to Philip. During the past two months in which she had spent a part of each day with her lover, she had grown confident; they were both happy. Isabel no longer feared for the man beginning his fresh career. For his book—at last finished—had been sent to an Eastern publisher. Philip had not heard definitely, but there was reason to believe that the house in question would be glad to bring out a finely illustrated work on cathedrals which might readily appeal to a cultured class of readers. Already Isabel felt elated over her lover's beginning. The field of letters seemed more choice, more set apart, since Philip had decided to compete for honors. In imagination she saw her future husband's prolific volumes. How proudly she would dust the dark green row marked "Barry." She remembered that the name was preëmpted by a master Scotch novelist, and decided that "Philip Barry" should appear in full on the backs of the new author's uniform edition. She had read only parts of her lover's work, but it had been exciting to handle a real manuscript, one which must go forth to win! Philip alone understood the uncertain odds against disappointment. In a fight for fresh life he felt no desire for anything but honest work. The book had started upon a journey East a month before, and now each day Isabel watched her lover's face for news of its unqualified acceptance.

The collection of exquisite cathedral views—actual paintings—done in Paris and submitted by a noted artist, would doubtless enhance the value of the work, yet it was, after all, Philip's part which timed the woman's heart to feverish interest. And to-day was her wedding day. From now on the book and its author were both hers. She stirred lightly in bed, again looking through the open flaps of her canvas room. A wonderful world was at last awake. Every bird evoked gladness, and Isabel too was glad. Then suddenly the boy slipped from his cot to snuggle within her arms. Enchantment of sleep lurked around his dewy eyes, and night had brushed his rounded cheeks with cool, fresh bloom. He kissed his mother again and again. "You've got most a bushel!" he cried. "Now I is going to love you." He was speaking more plainly each day, gradually ceasing to be a baby. "I like to stay with mother dear—in this nice bed," he said, contentedly. His arms held tighter. The mother's heart felt chill; she seemed to be turning the boy away. The child's words hurt her as she had never dreamed they could. She began to speak of a pony about to arrive, which she had purposely withheld against a trying time to come. "To-day is the day for the pony!" she announced bravely. "Mother's boy is to go out in his new cart with madame, is to drive like a man all afternoon."

"But I want mother dear to come too," the child insisted.

"Mother dear will come another day; to-day she is obliged to go to church, and then——" her voice failed. She had given her boy no idea of the change actually at hand, had weakly depended on accident and his love for Philip. How now could she make the little fellow understand? She began again. "To-day mother must go to church, and——"

"Will Philip dear go too?" the boy asked eagerly.

"Yes," said Isabel, glad of an opening wedge.

"And will the little bell ring?"

Isabel despaired. Would Reginald never forget? The Catholic services which he had once witnessed were yet vivid, and despite effort to dissociate Barry with a priest's part, the child was not well pleased with the conventional garb of his adored friend. Recently he had innocently inquired for the "bu-ti-ful hat" formerly worn before the altar. The boy's regret was so genuine that Philip felt his pale cheeks deepen. The mother had tactfully explained that "Father Barry" of old no longer preached in a church, and that now "Philip dear" had come to stay. The little boy, without understanding, adopted the change, and "Philip dear" had soon become both his playfellow and his teacher.

This morning Isabel tried in vain to pass over the hard part of a day that after all could not be happy until she had settled an important matter.

"Sweetheart," she implored, then flushed. "Precious boy, listen. Don't ask any more questions and mother will tell you all about the pony." Reginald placed his small hand over his mouth.

"I'm doing to keep stiller," he promised.

"Very well," said Isabel, pressing him to her heart. "The pony is sure to come right after luncheon. Mother may be away, but madame and Carolyn will both be here. Reggie must be very good and drive like a man all afternoon in his cart. Perhaps when madame has gone for a ride Carolyn will take her place and stop for little Elizabeth. Would not that be fine?"

"Great!" said Reginald; then added, "I suppose she'll have to bring every one of her dolls."

"Why not?"

"Oh, well, don't you see, so many dolls would take so much room? Then Elizabeth says I've got to be her husband."

"Why not?" said his mother, laughing.

"Because—because I just want to be your husband." He cuddled closer. Isabel wept miserably in his curls.

"Don't, oh, don't!" she pleaded. She smothered the boy with kisses until he cried out for release. Then she sat up in bed with the child in her arms. "Reginald, darling, you must listen. Mother is going to be married to Philip dear, to-day, at the church." She hurried on before the astonished boy could speak. "After mother is married to Philip dear, Reggie will have a kind father to love him, to take care of him always."

"Will he be 'Father Barry' again?" the boy inquired eagerly.

"No, no," she hastened to explain, "just father—Reggie's dear father."

"I think it will be nice," the boy acknowledged. He was still for a long time, with his cheek against his mother's. Isabel had not intended taking the child to church, but suddenly she changed her mind.

"Would Reggie like to come? Like to see mother married to Philip dear?" The questions fell gently, but the boy sprang up, shouting.

"May I?" he cried, with true desire to remember his manners. "Oh, may I? May I? Mother darling—goody! goody! goody!"

"I think you may," she answered.

He kept repeating, "Goody! goody!" Then all at once he grew sober. Something still troubled him. "Will Philip dear be your father, too?" he demanded.

"No darling, not my father, only my husband."

He waited a moment, evidently sifting the whole matter. His full baby lips trembled. "Will Philip dear be your husband all the time?" he asked. His mother nodded. "Then I suppose Elizabeth will make me be her husband." He heaved a little sigh which was masculine resignation personified. "Well, I don't care!" he exclaimed valiantly, "for you see, mother dear, I'm going to have a father and a pony, too. Goody! goody! goody!"

Chapter 19

Everything was at last arranged, and Carolyn dressed the boy for his mother's wedding. The little fellow looked proud and sober in his best white suit, with a tiny bunch of Isabel's forget-me-nots for a bridal favor. He sat very still and grown up all the way to the church, built after an English model and picturesquely hidden among green hills. The beautiful chapel made a complete surprise when the carriage stopped on the country road. Madame took Reginald's tiny gloved hand and led him forward, while Isabel moved slowly after them. As all three entered the church, bells began to sound, and a man came quickly forward to say that an Episcopal clergyman and Philip Barry were both waiting at the foot of the chancel. Madame guided her charge to a stall used by choir boys now absent. Here the old French woman and the boy stood, expectant. Isabel came on alone, vaguely conscious of her way; then suddenly she felt protected—loved, for Philip had reached her side. The clergyman entered the chancel. The man and woman to be joined in wedlock heard him begin the service. His words fell distinctly, and soon Isabel and Philip listened to the solemn charge administered before marriage. "That if either of you know any impediment why ye may not be lawfully joined together in matrimony, ye do now confess it," rang over their heads, into their souls, with momentary, questioning force. But the pause enjoined by the Church ended, and no voice had accused the apostate priest. The clergyman went on. Glad that the stern proviso was passed, Isabel faintly smiled, then glanced at Philip. He was pale. Undaunted, she put her hand in his and followed his deep responses with a clear voice. It seemed natural that he should remember the bar to their earlier happiness. Isabel moved slowly to the altar. By the side of the man she trusted she felt no fear. The sunlight of human love, the influence of home, a chance for intellectual freedom,—all these should make Philip forget a miserable, restless year. And at last the two were kneeling. Prayers and the benediction had made them one. The first test was over. Soon they were signing the parish register and could now leave the sacristy. The boy and madame were waiting. Again the bells sounded. Philip led the way to the carriage, and a moment later all were driving off together. Along the wayside early poppies lifted golden chalices to nuptial health, while a meadow lark extolled the day. All about, buzzing insects piped joy. Isabel was glad that she had selected the tiny country chapel for her marriage.

And the drive home was a pleasant one. Restraint lifted as the boy prattled and madame overflowed in French. Isabel and Philip gave out to each other without fear or confusion. Then came the gay arrival, with servants waiting, and the boy's pony and cart in readiness for a time postponed. But the mother no longer dreaded temporary parting, for now she was sure of her little son's will power. Since the confidence of early morning her heart had felt free. Throughout luncheon she planned for the boy's amusement during a month set apart for the honeymoon. There was much to be said about letters and surprises which were to arrive each day. Then when "mother dear" came back Reginald must drive her out into the country. Later the advent of kites would afford opportunity for an indulgent new father. The child was altogether satisfied. Isabel found no difficulty in slipping above for a change she had almost feared to make. When she came down dressed for traveling her son was so happy with his pony and cart that the equipage marking a bride's departure seemed to be purely incidental to the main interest of the afternoon.

With quick embraces, a farewell hand wave, Isabel and Philip were gone. The old slipper, flung by madame, hit the carriage and fell to the ground.

Chapter 20

At last!" said Philip; and his wife responded with a happy smile. The afternoon trip to St. Barnabas had begun. The two were sitting in the Pullman, at liberty to forget everything in the world but their wedding journey. As yet it was too soon to regard the future; the present was all satisfying. Isabel began to speak of their marriage ceremony, as most brides are apt to do. "How simple and easy it all was," she declared. "I shall always love that darling chapel among the hills. Did you feel the spring coming through the open windows? And did you hear the meadow lark on our way back? Oh, I loved it all."

Her husband smiled at her natural joy. Then peering into Philip's face Isabel saw again that his cheeks were thin. If anything he was more distinguished looking, yet already she feared for his health. He had been working too hard, and the next month must do wonders for the man she loved. "At St. Barnabas we shall live out of doors every moment of the day," she declared. "I can hardly wait to show you that wonderful country. It will be perfect to go about in the saddle; how glad I am that we sent the horses on ahead and in full time."

"You are a fairy wife instead of a fairy godmother," said Philip.

"Nonsense," she answered. "I am absolutely selfish. I love the saddle far better than my dinner, and my only fear is that I may tire you out."

"No danger; I'm going to astonish you. Besides, you have given me the easiest horse."

She denied the charge. "One is as fine a mount as the other. I shall never cease to be thankful to our friend Cole. And isn't it nice that he is to take care of the horses during our stay at the hotel?"

"Pretty nice for him," said Philip.

"And for us, too," she persisted. "I really did not wish to leave madame and Reginald without a coachman. Of course I could have let Tom come, but he is altogether too fond of a good time. Parker threatens to find another groom every week. Besides," she hesitated, then laughed, "besides, I wanted Cole and his little wife to have a treat. They will both enjoy getting away from the foothills."

"I called you a good fairy, now I am sure of it," said her husband. She smiled.

"Of what use is an income if we may not enjoy it?"

"Absolutely good for nothing," he answered.

"And it's almost selfishness to do little favors that in reality cost only the thought. Some day we must do something big—found an art institute, perhaps on this very coast." She was thinking of his lost cathedral. "Then I should love to help talented young girls with no way of reaching 'head waters.'" He looked at her proudly. "There are so many things needed—so many appeals to choose from, that we will surely find the right place for a little money." Philip remembered the check which she had sent him over a year ago.

Now her desire to make the whole world glad was part of her new happiness. But soon they talked of other matters, or else looked out through the wide window at charming, changing landscape. All afternoon the train climbed the rugged coast range, often boring its way through a tunneled mountain. At five o'clock they had tea on a small table, when a wonderful sunset touched every hill and spur of their upland road. Evening came all too soon. Stars began to peep, and suddenly domestic lights twinkled across a populous valley. Then, near by, the great Pacific beat eternal measure on silver sands. It was eight o'clock when the train stopped in St. Barnabas, at the rear of a noted caravansary flaming electrical welcome. Philip had already engaged rooms. Resigning his checks and suit cases to a waiting porter, he led Isabel down the footpath through a garden of palms and flowers. The way seemed fairyland, while on either hand the breath of blossoms filled the night.

"My wife—my precious wife," he said softly. At their feet stretches of shasta daisies lay as snow. Isabel pressed her husband's arm.

"Could any place be more perfect for our honeymoon?" she asked.

Lapping of waves reached the garden. The newly wed pair did not hasten, yet all too soon the flower-bordered path ended beneath lighted arches. The two went slowly forward, while just how to pass unconcernedly from the clerk's desk to the elevator, made them really seem like "bride and groom." For the first time each secretly acknowledged happy, bewildered self-consciousness. The blazing corridor filled with beautifully gowned women and men in evening dress, groups of older people back from an early dinner, strains of music calling late diners to waiting tables, gave instant local color to both time and place. Philip scrawling personal decoration on the hotel daybook grew careful and wrote the new appendage to his name with telltale neatness. However, it was soon over. Neither looking to right nor left the couple bolted past groups of curious women, were all but safe in the protecting elevator, when a familiar voice spoke Isabel's name. Gay

Lewis, alert for sensation, faced the grating of the rising lift. "Delighted to see you!" she called after them. And Philip Barry's wife answered with the smile prescribed under all conditions for a bride.

As they rose above, Philip looked questioningly at Isabel. "An old school friend of mine," she told him. He made a wry face.

"Have you many more of them about the hotel?" She laughed softly.

"I cannot say. One never knows whom one may meet in California."

They were leaving the elevator, following a boy with keys to their rooms. "I hope we shall not be surprised on every side," the man persisted. Isabel caught his hand.

"Never mind," she whispered, "I'll take care of you. But you must be nice to Gay Lewis. We are simply destined to meet the world over, and Gay has a way of saying things." The bell boy was beyond hearing distance. "Not that she has anything to say about us of slightest interest to strangers," she hastened to add. Philip saw the flush on her cheeks. Was she already beginning to dread unavoidable notoriety? The thought sobered him. Now he understood. But Isabel should not suffer, if being polite to every one in Christendom could help matters.

"I shall bend to 'the higher criticism,' do my best to impress Miss Lewis," he declared with assumed gayety.

Then Isabel exclaimed as the door to their spacious sitting-room flew open. The place was a bower of roses. "Did you tell them to do it?" she asked.

Philip forgot a passing shadow and smiled an affirmative answer.

"It is lovely! the loveliest room I was ever in," she declared. "How dear of you." Philip stopped by the window, enjoying his wife's girlish joy. She sank her face into every separate bunch of flowers. "Oh, these dear, dear pink ones!" she cried.

American Beauties nodded above her head, and she stood on a footstool to inhale their fragrance. On a round table covered with a white cloth was a huge bowl of "bride roses," fitting emblem for the day. Philip's surprise had been perfect. The delicate forethought which had ordered her bower, which stipulated for the little dinner to be served in the sitting-room, away from curious eyes, touched her beyond words. Her husband was indeed a lover! She ran to him with outstretched arms. As never before she knew the depth of a long-denied moment. And later, when she laid aside her coat and hat, to sit at the first little dinner alone,—but for the deferential waiter coming in and going out,—she kept thinking of all that they had in store, of their happiness to come.

Philip was never as gay, never so like the boy of years back—the boy who had loved the girl. Both were beginning over again and time between had taught them the price of joy.

"On this night we toast each other," said Philip, lifting his glass. "There is just 'one cold bottle' for our 'little hot bird'! I drink to my wife!"

His eyes glowed. Isabel touched his glass with her own. "To the dearest husband in the whole big world!" she responded, then kissed him. He held her away from him, feasting on her beauty. But she begged for freedom, and took her place at the opposite side of the table. "We must behave," she cautioned. "He's coming! I hear him down the hall."

"I will be circumspect," Philip promised. "But I'm losing my appetite. I don't feel glad of salad and the rest. Let's fire him before the coffee; I want to sip mine with my wife on my knee."

"For shame!" she chided, as the waiter tapped the door, with a loaded tray. "Do seem to be hungry. If we send things back untouched we shall be the talk of the hotel kitchen." Laughter was a natural part of the little dinner. "It is just like playing party," she declared, when the man again disappeared.

"Please pass the sugar," Philip begged. "Won't you kiss me again?"

"Not now," she refused. "We must remember that Reginald is learning table manners; if we act too badly through our honeymoon, he may notice shortcomings when we get home. Besides, he's coming—the waiter's coming. Be dignified."

"Will coffee ever begin?" Philip complained.

"Very soon." They both laughed.

"Which shall I use, a fork or a spoon for my frozen pudding?"

"Your fork—by all means; now please talk sensibly; he's just outside."

Philip thought of the king who dined without servants, and wished that he too had built a table for the occasion, one with a dummy lift in its center, to bring up food and to carry away the dishes.

Isabel watched with playful eyes until the last of his pudding was gone. Then she dismissed the waiter. Black coffee and a first cigar for the benedict state were both enjoyed without interruption. The evening lengthened. Philip saw his wife flit about the rooms with joyous air of proprietorship. Reginald's picture stood on the table beside the "bride roses."

Something told him to go below on a natural pretext, for their trunks were late. When he went out Isabel did not stir. Everything was so wonderful, so much more wonderful than she had fancied. But at last she began to move about, smiling. She hung her traveling coat in the closet and brushed her hat. Her suit case was unlocked and unstrapped, and she drew forth things which were needed. She loosened her hair, plaiting it as usual. Two golden braids hung down her back. Then she slipped into a soft robe of silk and lace, and stood by the window facing the sea, waiting for her husband.

Chapter 21

Philip and Isabel spent much time in the saddle. Heavy rains of the season had suspended, leaving the country fresh and fragrant. Heather-toned effects on mountains round about, the sky so azure that the depths of blue seemed immeasurable, drew the newly wedded pair each morning. They always found Cole waiting with their horses. It soon grew to be an event for less favored guests of the hotel to watch the couple mount, then gallop off. Isabel had no suspicion of the incessant comment created by her slightest public movement. With Philip it was different. But for his wife's complete satisfaction he would have chosen a retreat on the foothills above the sea. He knew of such a place, and longed to leave the crowded hotel, where all were talking behind his back, whispering of his abolished priesthood, impugning his motives, testing his action by opposing scales of ignorant enthusiasm and bitter prejudice. For he constantly heard unguarded remarks, felt the prick of gossip as he passed from one place to another. Isabel was all unconscious of her husband's sensitive state. For Philip had kept his word, treating Gay Lewis, and in fact every one whom he met, with due consideration. Miss Lewis hung on his slightest word, while at the same time she established Isabel with an elect coterie of young wives whose husbands played tennis or polo at the hotel country club. Afternoons were often passed in watching sports in the open. Sometimes Philip and Isabel cantered into the club grounds in time for a simple luncheon; frequently they joined new acquaintances at table. Then again they sat apart by themselves, relaxing after a long ride through the valley or on the wonderful mountain road as yet undesecrated by automobiles. For at St. Barnabas the ubiquitous motor car is somewhat restrained. The famous mountain drive is still a tradition and sacred to the family carriage and "happy tots" on ponies. Philip and Isabel never grew tired of walking their horses around curves, which made the winding way a panorama of sky, mountains, valley, and sea. "There is nothing more lovely in the world!" Isabel would exclaim each time they left the upland for the return sweep past beautiful villas and gardens. Then came a gallop by the ocean. But on other days they took a different direction, going past "The Mission," riding, as it were, beyond the pale of sacred history into territory where heretics alone might disregard the murmured prayers of monks. It was strange how the work of the old fathers dominated the landscape. At points the mission held the skyline, and on every side its twin towers proclaimed the beauty of simple strength. To the man cast out from Catholic favor there was inanimate reproach in every elemental line of the early church. Against the blue a perspective of pure Spanish architecture fascinated him. His thoughts went out—against his will—to the cathedral he had longed to perpetuate. Romish emotion, fostered at birth, imbibed with his pious mother's milk, rose unbidden;—a challenge to his love for Isabel. His wife always seemed to conquer, and he stifled the dread that threatened as he turned his back on the mission. Then suddenly it loomed once more. Again he felt its compelling powers, its binding simplicity. Meanwhile, no suspicion of Philip's struggle entered Isabel's mind, for her own keen delight in the church was serene. The mission to her was an esthetic opportunity, a relic that a comparatively new world ought to be proud of. She was a purist in art, and after a second visit to St. Barnabas she loved every line of the historic mission. Yet she had not asked her husband to go inside of a now forbidden place. She longed to enjoy once more the marvelous view from the twin towers, but as doing so would involve Philip, she had given up the idea. Their honeymoon was already perfect. Each day she felt happier, more certain that she had been wise to marry Philip. Once she marveled at a young priest's power; now the man—her husband—held her with the same irresistible fascination. For Philip was a wonderful lover, both implied and manifest. And besides, after a fortnight's trial, Isabel pronounced him the most charming comrade. Also, there were moments when the two felt willing for a silent interval, when neither one spoke or demanded attention. It was at such times only that Philip unconsciously brooded over the ecclesiastical tragedy of his life.

But Isabel blindly rejoiced in her husband's balance, while each gay canter past the mission brought fresh assurance of his good sense. Then suddenly one morning he asked her to dismount for an interior view of the old church. She did not hesitate. It seemed manly, natural, that he should be strong enough to put aside personal feeling, should be able to enjoy an esthetic opportunity at hand. And she shrewdly divined that he was tired of denying his interest in the supreme tourist sight of the locality. By going through the mission his noticeable attitude might be changed. She had no appreciation of his risk from the Catholic standpoint. As she walked forward by his side she felt neither embarrassment nor fear. After all, they were both strangers, coming with thousands of others who looked, departed, and left an offering of money. The gold of heretics had really restored the mission. The man once a priest led his wife beneath an historic arch of the long gallery. Here the two stopped. Three brown-cloaked monks sat on a bench enjoying the sun.

"We should like to go through the mission," said Philip.

The oldest "brother" of the trio arose. "You are welcome," he answered pleasantly.

The two younger monks got up quickly, passed before the visitors, crossed a whitewashed anteroom, unlocked a solid door, then sprung it back in the face of oncoming Isabel. But despite the haste of a fleeing order she had caught a glimpse of the sacred garden beyond, and it did not occur to her disqualified judgment to regard herself as a natural temptation for carnal thoughts. She simply smiled at the rude opportunity enjoined by holiness. As she followed the "brother" in charge of the regulation tour for strangers, she kept wondering about the tall, handsome monk who had used a pass key on the spring lock of the oaken door.

He was a splendid specimen of manhood, and Isabel could still see his fine head, his modeled jaw and chin, the strong mouth; above all, the swinging freedom of his limbs underneath his rough brown habit. She regretted the unattractive personality of the attending brother, yet at the same time she tried—as she always tried—to repay a debt with simple gratitude. It was soon plain that the austere monk regarded her with favor.

As they went from one small whitewashed room to another, pausing to examine some rude relic of early mission days, Isabel led in the conversation. "It is all very interesting," she declared. "And the church has been so consistently restored," she went on. "I do not wonder that you are proud of the only mission in California which has not been treated to some shocking innovation. Even the dear old church at San Gabriel has taken on a modern redwood ceiling utterly devoid of art's religion."

The brother's thin lips drew apart in a quizzical smile. "You must become a Catholic and help us to preserve the crumbling architecture of the good fathers," he suggested.

"I should love to help the work along," she answered. They had finished with the small, chilly, almost antiseptically treated rooms, open to strangers, and were now standing at the foot of the old stairway leading above to the towers. On account of previous experience Isabel regarded the high stone steps with trepidation. The brother, not intending to mount, bade them take their time, then meet him again outside in the sunshine. Philip offered to help his wife with an initial lift, but she refused assistance, declaring that to be game when mounting historic steps was the only way. "I may not be able to move to-morrow, but to-day I shall not think of future punishment," she gayly jested. Philip went behind to guard her as she took the penitential climb. And at last both were resting in the ancient belfry, close to the old bells from Spain. Below the sacred garden lay plain to their view. Philip pictured the first sinful man peering into forbidden Eden. Then he remembered that Adam still had Eve.

Chapter 22

Philip stood looking down, with his hand lightly resting on Isabel's shoulder. Beyond the fountain, before the timeworn cloister, sat an aged brother surrounded by monks. It was plain that the old brother was ill, perhaps nearing the end of a chosen life on earth, for he was speaking to the young monks, who seemed to hang on every word, hovering around his chair with awkward, masculine devotion. In all probability these same vigorous men would carry the old brother on his bier to the little cemetery, where he might displace the whitened bones of some monk long dead and forgotten.

As Philip gazed down on the scene below, translating as well he might the end of justified means to Catholic grace, his eyes filled with tears. For some unaccountable reason the dying monk suggested his mother. The reproach which she had never given him in life now seemed to ascend from the old garden—from the invalid brother leaning back on pillows. Philip turned away, and Isabel saw that he was hurt. Instantly her hand held his. "Let us go," she implored. But he smiled back refusal.

"I was just thinking of my mother," he confessed. "You must not forget that she was a Catholic, consistent and happy to the end of her days. I could not help associating her in my mind with the good brother below us. I have been told that an old monk has never been known to pass away with regret; only the young ones, sometimes, feel restless in the cloister."

He had not spoken in this manner before. Isabel covertly scanned his countenance. His cheeks held a slight hollow, almost imperceptible, except when his face was turned in a certain way. Standing with his back to the light, in the arch of the belfry, his eyes seemed too bright for normal condition. Isabel remembered the strain of his past year.

"Let us not climb above onto the roof," she pleaded. Still he would not forego the broader view, and helped her to cross from one tower to the other. As they halted, spellbound, to breathe mountain air, to drink salt breeze, Isabel again looked at her husband. He was smiling in sensuous pleasure. It came to her joyously that time alone could heal his wounded spirit. It seemed manly that he should be able to delight in his present environment without prejudice; that he should face phases of Catholic power without pain. It were preposterous to try to wipe out the realm of Romish influence; for to do that meant to give up "old world" cathedrals and universal art, inspired by popes and cardinals. Yes, Philip was wise to tread his new way freely as a free man.

But when they had descended from the tower Isabel stood undecided. "Are you sure that you wish to enter the church?" she asked.

Her husband hesitated, with eyes on the stone floor. The flashing recollection of an awful interdict held him; then he looked up. "I am no longer a Catholic," he acknowledged coldly. "I have the right to see the interior of the mission church, like any other American citizen. Come, let us hasten."

Isabel followed, dimly conscious of his defiant mood. The brother, waiting without, led them across ancient flagstones to timeworn steps of generous dimension. In fancy Philip saw flocking dark-faced Indians of early days mounting to service. The work of the unselfish fathers accused him even before he entered the fine old edifice; but he went on, with intent to stifle all but esthetic feeling. He felt relieved when his wife assumed a questioning attitude that was cordially appreciated by the brother in charge.

Here in the old church, by the side of a brown-habited monk, Isabel shone as usual. It became clear to Philip that his wife and not himself attracted their guide. He walked on, listening to the brother's story of early mission life and art, with no outward sign of inculcated knowledge. At every curtained confessional, before Spanish pictures of saints, at every sacred shrine, he told himself defiantly that he played no dishonorable part. The curious temper of the observer condoned his bold action. He was "a stranger within the gates." He went forward to the foot of the chancel as a man in a dream. That less than two years back he might have penetrated with full right beyond to the flower-dressed altar brought him a momentary pang, but he stifled it and looked at Isabel. Did she know—understand? Her serene face expressed no undercurrent of emotion. The reserve force of splendid womanhood had walled in her husband's past with natural, incidental, impersonal interest for everything at hand. Then, as they stood on listening to the brother's fervent account of work done by early mission Indians, notes from the organ broke the strain; while presently a baritone voice of wonderful quality floated below from the choir loft. Isabel turned in surprise. Even at the far end of the church she saw clearly the two young monks who had gone through the heavy door to the secret garden. The tall, lithe-limbed monk was the singer; his cloister brother accompanied him on the organ.

"How beautiful!" she exclaimed, sitting down by Philip, in a convenient pew. "They are practicing—for service?" she asked.

The brother in charge nodded. He seemed disappointed that his own rhetorical opportunity should be eclipsed by the mere song of a youngster. But the charming heretic no longer listened to a story of dark, slow-moving converts. Her eyes had ceased to rest on fantastic colored designs carved by early Indians and now transferred to the new wooden ceiling of the old church. The voice in the choir loft held her; and with a woman's will she chose to end the brother's attentions. Besides, Philip seemed worn with sacred tradition.

"We have enjoyed everything very much!" she said with enthusiasm. "If we may come another day for a glimpse of the old cemetery, we should now prefer to listen to the music." She smiled, one hand extended. As the brother hesitated she drew a goldpiece from her glove. When Philip too responded with natural impulse, the brown monk moved away. He turned once to look back, then went on. They caught the gleam in his eyes. After all, they had paid in full, were not intruders in the mission always open to a curious public.

Chapter 23

Philip and Isabel were in full time for luncheon. The wife noticed that her husband ate his toast and squab with appetite. His cheeks were flushed from the canter back to the hotel, while during the half hour at table he appeared both happy and talkative.

"Shall you mind if I go off this afternoon for golf?" he asked, as they went from the dining-room.

Isabel's face expressed satisfaction. Her husband had hardly left her side since their arrival. She believed in casual separation. She knew instinctively that Philip must feel renewed interest in his own sex, to be quite the man he had been before his trouble of months back.

"Go, by all means," she encouraged, as they went from the elevator to their rooms. "Golf must be your game; it will do you a world of good to follow the links."

"And you won't miss me?"

"Not a bit," she answered. "Besides, I want to expect you back. I wish to feel the pang of parting, so that I may know how very, very lonely I used to be." She spoke lightly, but he knew that in reality she did not jest. "And the man—your opponent in golf?" she asked.

Philip stooped and kissed her. "How do you know that I am not going to tread the turf with a fair lady?" he teased.

"I should be awfully jealous," she confessed. He knew that she spoke the truth. It came over him at the time that men were few who might claim such love as Isabel's. In her starry eyes he read salvation, felt the depth of her womanly will. Inadequate power to repay his debt made him humble. He kissed her again, holding her close with adoring tenderness. Then he told her that he was about to play golf with the great publisher whom he had recently met. The triumph on her lips amused him.

"Build no air-castles!" he begged. But she freed herself from his arms and danced like a child.

"What a chance!" she cried. "You must make him your friend. I saw last evening that he was immensely interested in you, and now he may ask you to write for his magazine." Isabel's estimate of her husband's genius, of his ability to rush into print in one of the foremost monthly publications in the country, was fresh proof of her blind passion.

"Don't think such foolish things, dear little girl," Philip commanded. "The road to solicited manuscripts is a long way off—as yet. I shall have to get my stuff back many, many times before I can count on an indulgent editor." He spoke humbly, yet withal the eternal spark of hope had kindled for his literary career.

"Shall you tell him of your book—about 'The Spirit of the Cathedral'?"

Philip shook his head. "That might frighten him. He would think that I had an ax to grind."

"But you have sent your manuscript to another publishing house," she persisted.

"That is true," he assented, "but until I hear definitely, I do not care to talk of my forthcoming book. Besides, the man is here for rest and change. If I am able to make him my friend he may possibly tell me things. Above all, I must not bore him with my own uncertain achievements." He laughed, tugging at his golf shoe. "But you shall try your art on the man this evening; I have promised to present him."

"I will do my best," Isabel answered. "And by reason of the dance to-night the bride may wear white satin. She is irresistible in la robe empire."

Philip faced her. "I see all my manuscripts accepted at once," he said jestingly.

"Of course. Now run along; do not keep our great man waiting. I shall rest for an hour, then write to madame and Reginald."

"And you are really able for a ball, after the high steps of the mission tower?"

It was the first time that he had spoken of their morning's experience. Isabel was overjoyed at his light reference to the visit to the old church.

"To dance will limber me, beyond doubt," she declared, with a wave of her hand. She watched him pass down the hall to the elevator; then she went back to her sitting-room.

At last she felt the glad sense of partnership. Ambition for the man she loved threatened to become more absorbing than all else in her life. Suddenly her boy seemed to reproach her. On the table his lifelike portrait begged for notice. She caught up the silver frame.

"Darling little son!" she murmured, "mother will soon be at home—more than ever your playmate, your companion." She put the picture down and sat with her head resting between her hands. Her thoughts were now all with Reginald. What was he doing? Was he out in his pony cart? Was dainty baby Elizabeth along, giving the dolls an airing? Then, above all, did the boy miss his "mother dear"? She drew a crumpled half sheet of paper from an envelope. "Bless his dear little heart," she again murmured. Reginald's zigzag message, together with round spots wonderfully colored to represent kisses, drew her lips. She responded to a realistic fancy, smiling above her son's confident masterpiece. Then she re-read a letter from madame. All were moving along, and the child was happy.

Her old friend's idiomatic expression kept her smiling to the end, while she realized anew the good fortune which had brought the French woman to California. In future Reginald might have every chance with his French. The mother decided to make luncheon, with the boy at table, a time set apart for French conversation. Philip, too, spoke the foreign tongue; and again Isabel planned for Reginald's liberal education. And she meant to study herself, by the side of a talented husband. How full life promised to become. But with every consistent hope her own ambition was subordinate to love. To love, to be loved by Philip, by Reginald, by friends, constituted the little world she longed to conquer. And to-night, she wished to shine at the ball, not as a woman evoking admiration from the crowd, but as Philip's wife. If she might help to bring him fresh power she was satisfied. Nor did Isabel deny her own evident advantage. She was too familiar with standards of beauty not to be glad of a rich inheritance; yet in all her life she had never been vain. For to be vain is to be selfish, pinned upon a revolving, personal pivot. Isabel had always thought first of others. To-day her mind was full of schemes for Philip, for Reginald, and for old madame. If Philip agreed she wished to live permanently in California. She had already put her closed house in the West on the market. The city which had once been home no longer claimed her interest. And Philip must never go back to the scene of his past humiliation. She reached for a traveling portfolio and began to write to Reginald. Here and there she pasted bright pictures to illustrate a little story which would be sure to delight her boy. When she had finished she dashed off a letter in French to madame; then, fearing that Philip might be late, she laid out his dinner clothes. She was not in need of companionship, and a couch close to the wide window facing the sea lured her. She would rest. Waves splashed a rhythm of contentment. Out beyond the breakers a buoy creaked in vain, for her nerves were as sound as her boy's. She did not mind the incessant grind. She was happy—satisfied.

Chapter 24

The Saturday evening hop, which so often was a perfunctory recurrence, blossomed into an occasion, when a score of United States naval officers entered the hotel. The great fleet had not then made the gallant dash around the Horn; but for several years preceding this noted achievement stray battleships had touched along the Western coast. The ship in question bound for Manila was now anchored over night outside the breakers of St. Barnabas. Corridors of the hotel palpitated when privileged men off the man-of-war burst upon the scene. In less than a minute maneuvers in the ballroom eclipsed those of the outlying battleship, as anxious mammas steered young daughters to open port. Lines drew taut and merciless for all untouched by the accolade of station, while on every side sat groups of elderly onlookers.

Officers in immaculate evening dress, ready for change, eager to dance with pretty women, moved easily about, and soon surcharged conditions were overcome by general satisfaction.

By Isabel's side Gay Lewis shone with reflected prominence. Nor did the girl deny the evident truth when flocking ensigns marked her for second choice.

"You are a dear!" she reiterated after each opportunity due to her friend. "I have not had a chaperone for a long time. Now I see my blunder." For Philip Barry's wife was the undoubted toast of the navy men.

In a day when dancing has degenerated into pathetic uncertainty the advent of willing ensigns might well be put down as something new and exhilarating. Isabel forgot her strenuous climb to the mission roof. She had not enjoyed a ball for full five years; and she was like a girl surrounded by a swarm of admirers. To-night the great publisher had no chance, with epaulets to right and left. But the afternoon at golf had been successful. Philip and his new friend stood together on the outskirts, each duly conscious of his own inadequate worth.

"It behooves us to tread modestly—we fellows who have adopted a sober career," the editor declared. "I never could learn. My mother kept me at dancing school until I had tramped the toes of every little girl in the class, then one day she gave me up." He laughed drolly, while his eyes took in the swift, unconscious movement of Mrs. Barry and her partner, a tall young ensign.

"We are not in China, and fortunately I may speak to you of your wife," he went on. "As a comparatively new acquaintance, I beg to congratulate you. You are too fortunate in a world where many are not."

Barry stiffened. The other sensed misapprehension.

"I have never been married," he explained. "I am denied the pleasure of admiring my own wife. Those days at dancing school took away all possible hope. For years I could hardly shake hands with a girl of my own age; then you see I got wedded to single life—spent my days passing upon loves of fictitious heroes and heroines."

"Too bad," said Philip, deeply interested.

"Sometimes I think I should have made a much better judge of literature if I had only asked a woman to share my criticisms and bear my remorse when I turn down very readable things. You see a man who has not married can never be quite as sure as one who knows the taste of both good and evil. 'The woman which thou gavest me' may do a lot of mischief, but when the crash comes she generally compensates. For my part I doubt if Adam would have gone back into the garden with any interest whatever after Eve found 'pastures new' outside."

"And you believe that a married man is capable of better work than a single one?" Philip was growing curious.

"Undoubtedly," the editor answered. "I have in my mind a certain writer of note, one who but for persistent bachelorhood might have risen to highest rank in fiction. As it is, he has always fallen short of the real emotion. A certain class reading his books fail to detect mere description in supposedly passionate episodes, but to those of deeper consciousness and experience he has counterfeit feeling. This particular novelist works from matrimonial patterns—traces all that he draws. I am older than yourself, and you will pardon me for saying it, but your wife should help you to achieve almost anything."

Philip flushed. The pride of possession came over him afresh when Isabel whirled past, with a smile which he knew could never be untrue. Above her radiance, beauty, he felt her exquisite womanhood. To-night he believed that she would lead him to "pastures new—outside." Throughout the evening Philip stayed by the editor, gradually making his way into the man's confidence, while adhering to a first determination which withheld the fact of his own unprinted book. Then at midnight, Isabel, Miss Lewis, and three young officers captured the onlookers and forced them away to supper.

It was a gay little party. The round table at which all sat became an excuse for a full hour's enjoyment; and as Isabel had promised, she did her best to make the editor, who might possibly help Philip, her own friend also. The undertaking was not difficult. If dancing school trials had left an eternal scar on the bachelor's unclaimed heart to-night he showed no unwillingness to devote himself to Isabel. Philip was amused. Then he remembered his wife's unfailing charm. He had never seen her unsympathetic or rude. When she really cared to please, she could not be soon forgotten by any one selected for her favor. And to-night, as usual, the elderly publisher and the young ensigns from the ship all went under to a woman's gracious way. Nor was Miss Lewis annoyed.

"Of course," she said afterward, "no one ever attempts to eclipse Isabel; for don't you see she would not care in the least, and that being the case, no other woman would be foolish enough to try—and then fail." And Gay was at her best during supper. Philip had never liked her as well as when the party broke up. There was, after all, something fine and straightforward about the girl, who appeared to drift with the tide of hotel pastimes. Philip told himself that as a priest he had been narrow in many of his judgments. The evening had stimulated his respect for the world. His emotional nature went out again to things he had once given up. Isabel's beauty held him in passionate bonds; and he felt incentive for new work. His book, which came next to his wife—for no one writes seriously without the sense of humanized accomplishment—suddenly went up in his own estimation. The evening with a real publisher had stiffened his confidence; and for the first time since his marriage he merged love for Isabel with the success of "The Spirit of the Cathedral." But his personal undercurrent passed unnoticed. To his wife he seemed detached from all but the present. As she drew him away from the shining ballroom she exulted to herself. Unusual and lighter opportunity seemed to be what her husband most needed.

The battleship hauled anchor at dawn. The men had already started for the tug and a trip across the breakers. The hotel was despoiled of glory. Corridors were soon dim and lonely. To Isabel the night had proved her husband's ease with a life comparatively new and untried. She felt young, contented, ready for all which might come. Not a fear for Philip crossed her mind as she went to her rooms. She had been exhilarated throughout the evening; but now she was glad to rest. Philip unfastened her gown, halting to kiss her bare shoulders, to tell her about their friend, the magazine editor. As she slipped out of her ball finery she was like a girl after a first night of conquest. Later he listened to her gentle, regular breathing as he lay by her side. It seemed yet a dream that she was really his wife. Events of the past began to fill his mind. Then reaction, which so often came with excess of feeling, kept him awake for hours. But at last he dropped away, only to rouse up at intervals. The outgoing tide seemed to carry him to the anchored ship, gleaming beyond. The incessant, yet broken passion of the sea forbade sleep. With every tardy lap of waves he grew more restless; and dawn broke. All at once, a desire to witness the departure of the man-of-war drew him from bed. Isabel slumbered as a child, and Philip went softly to the window and looked out. The sea rose and fell an arctic green. There was no mist, and he could see the great ship clearly. A streamer of black smoke floated across the morning sky; already there were signs of departure. Philip dressed quickly and quietly. It occurred to him that Isabel might be shocked to awaken and find him gone. He smiled as he slipped into the sitting-room to indite a line "To the Sleeping Beauty." But his wife did not stir when he pinned the note to his own empty pillow. He went back to the adjoining apartment for his field glasses; then out of the door through quiet halls, to a side entrance below, where he found an open way.

Chapter 25

Philip watched the maneuvers of the battleship from the shore, at the foot of the hotel. His glasses were strong, and he could make out regular disciplined movements of men on board. What a life, he thought. To be always waiting for war, ready for action in any part of the world, regardless of human personal ties. The monster breasting waves seemed as horrible as it was majestic. The man who was once a priest had never wished to be a soldier. This morning he sensed the command to draw anchor, felt the significance of carnage for the sea, saw the ship move. Against a skyline, clear with oncoming day, it took unchallenged sway. The man followed with his glasses. He stood fascinated by almost imperceptible motion. Against morning sky a black streamer rested, then gradually trailed to invisible distance, as broadside perspective dropped away. The man-of-war was gone. But Philip still stood on the shore. Early day had taken possession of his will. He seemed rooted to the wet sand beneath his feet. Was Isabel awake? Had she yet missed him? He looked back at the hotel, rising above lawn and palm trees. He could see no signs of life, and it occurred to him that a brisk walk might atone for his restless night. The fresh air stimulated him as he went forward. Without thought of destination he left the ocean for the esplanade, the esplanade for the long business street of the town. As he went on he began to see people and to realize for the first time that it was Sunday. Many were going to early Mass, and he was not among them. At a corner he saw a modern Catholic church. The old mission now had its rival in the new brick building. Several maids from the hotel got off a car to hurry onward. A woman in front went faster as she neared the church, but turned half round and looked at Philip. He felt her insinuating survey as he strode rapidly away; then he recognized Reginald Doan's former nurse. It was undoubtedly Maggie; and she knew him for all that he had once been. He could not be mistaken. That Maggie had deceived Isabel and followed Mrs. Grace to St. Barnabas was plain. With that lady's departure for the East, the girl must have ceased to be her maid. Maggie's surprise seemed evident; and at best the encounter was disagreeable. Philip hurried on with the sense of being watched. He walked past gardens, not seeing flowers freshened by night's cool touch and morning's breath. Suddenly he was cast down, depressed by something impalpable.

But he went on and on in absent-minded mood, taking no note of locality, not realizing his distance from the closely settled town. He followed the track of a car line, dimly conscious of the way, until, without warning—the mission faced him. He might have known! Still he had the habit of losing himself when Isabel was not his leader; and they seldom went out except on their horses. Miserable, angry, he stood afar, irresistibly called by sounding bells.

He saw men and women go up the wide worn steps to early Mass; then like an outcast he turned away to board a car returning to the hotel. Isabel would be waiting, wondering what had become of him. And he would not tell her, would never let her know of his childish trip. The mission had become an obsession. He saw it in his dreams and heard about it on all sides. Every artist painted it; and carriage drivers on the streets urged him to take a seat for the inevitable trip. Children showed him their post cards adorned with a picture of the historic church or else some scene taken in the cloister garden. The mission was getting onto his nerves. He was almost beginning to hate it. He would never see it again; and with the thought, he looked back at the graceful stretch of the low, sun-kissed monastery, following on like a little brother to the close protection of the "old fathers'" abler work. It was so beautiful, so simple, that he could not deny. His knowledge of architecture, his sense of fitness, kept his thoughts with the unselfish monks of the past. He could not forget when from boyhood he had been trained in church history. He had always been best in his class. And how his dear mother would have loved the old church. At last the car was moving; at last he might get away.

His back was to the mission and the run to town would not take long. After all he might not be very late. And as he had hoped, he found the hotel still quiet. Only a few early risers were down for breakfast when he went to the dining-room to order Isabel's tray sent up to her room. Then he took the elevator. He entered by the same door through which he had departed, walking softly to his wife's bedside. She seemed not to have stirred during his absence; but the note was gone from the pillow. He leaned down and kissed her, and at the same instant half bare arms tightened around his neck. Then she laughed.

"'Sleeping Beauties' never wake up unless they are kissed," she told him. He doubled his charm as she raised on her elbow.

"Did you think I was never coming back?" he asked. "I took a long walk, after the ship got away, went farther than I intended."

"I thought so," she said. "Men never remember the return trip. But I have hardly missed you. I read my love letter, then went right to sleep. I did not wake until I heard the telephone. Of course I answered it, and whom do you suppose was speaking?"

"Doubtless one of your numerous admirers," her husband gallantly answered.

"No. This time it was your admirer. But I came in for honorable mention. I am so flattered, almost glad that you were not here to respond to our friend the editor."

Now she was wide awake. The soft disarrangement of night still hung about her hair. Her eyes sparkled as the morning. She sat up, leaning forward.

"He has invited us to go out with him this afternoon in his touring car. I said we would come. You are willing?"

"Of course," Philip answered, smiling at her eagerness.

"Mr. and Mrs. Tilton-Jones and Gay Lewis are asked; we are to start about three."

Philip puckered his brow. "Why the Tilton-Joneses—I wonder?" Isabel saw that he did not care for the couple.

"They are relatives of our host," she explained. "One cannot turn down cousins in California, or for that matter, acquaintances. You must be nice to them, for last night both expressed the wish to know you." She was anxious for her husband's popularity with strangers. That he should hold his new place without criticism was always in her mind.

Isabel knew the world, and when she married an apostate priest she had considered its way, all outside of love. She had even prepared herself for first, almost inevitable rebuff. Time would show where she and Philip both stood. A desirable few, who obstinately disapproved, should not annoy her; and at last they too might forget. To her surprise she had felt no condemnation. A mere marriage notice passed from paper to paper, with miraculous decency. Isabel read no highly colored version of either her own beauty or of Philip's sensational conduct. If anything unpleasant appeared she did not see it. This morning as she sat up in bed, enjoying the breakfast which her husband had thoughtfully ordered, she was more than thankful, more than happy.

Chapter 26

And you do not care for the Tilton-Jones combination?" she asked.

Philip shook his head. "I fail to admire either of them, although I least of any one should cast a presumptuous stone. Perhaps I am unduly prejudiced. I have known several hyphenated Jones people before, and for some reason I never got on with them. You see I was always addressing the wife as plain Mrs. Jones—perpetually overlooking the lean-to addition."

Isabel's laugh rippled. How very clever her husband was. "I shall keep you from forgetting this afternoon," she promised. "I am so glad to go out in a machine. Really I do not believe I could sit the saddle to-day. And this is too nice!" she declared, as she poured the coffee. "Are you not going down?" Then she extended a steaming cup. "Take this," she begged. "They have sent plenty for two; suppose we have breakfast together."

"But there is only one cup."

"What matter, when we have a full pot of coffee. And just see the toast and rolls."

Philip sat facing his wife, amused as he always was when he had only to obey.

"You drink first," she commanded.

"Tell me when to stop; I might take all."

"You may. I never really enjoy coffee until I have finished."

She was irresistible. And all this loveliness, this unconsciousness, was now but for his own eyes. Isabel was his wife. To-day he felt that he had sinned only by once becoming a priest bound by unnatural vows.

God had created a pair in the beginning, decreed that man should not live without sympathy, without love. He was thinking of couples bound as prisoners. Everything seemed so natural for Isabel and himself, except when he did not sleep or went back too far. The white satin empire gown lay extended on the couch.

Philip pointed drolly across the room, then touched the sleeve of Isabel's dainty night robe. "I like this gown best; you seem about eighteen months, hardly old enough to be Reggie's fond mamma."

"For shame!" she cried. Still she was pleased. With mention of her boy she began to talk of the little fellow, to wonder what he was doing on this very Sunday morning.

The breakfast above proved to be a happy thought. Husband and wife "took turns" from the single cup; there was gayety and byplay.

"We have not left a crumb!" said Isabel. "I never ate such good toast. You know we are to have dinner at one—the regulation hour for the day; we shall subsist until then." She poured the last drop from the coffee pot. "This is our loving cup. Let us drink to every one that is married—in the big world!"

Philip smiled. "That wouldn't do, too many miss the whole thing," he answered.

"I suppose so," she agreed. She had almost forgotten the time when life had not been full and satisfying. "Now it is all so wonderful—so sure," she added softly.

"But of course honeymoons have got to be silly—real silly—just like this breakfast. After a while we shall both be serious enough, with your literary work and Reg growing up."

She bounded from bed to her dressing room, dropping Philip a courtesy in return for his previous jest. "I will come forth full grown," she promised. "Your friend the editor shall never suspect that I still love dolls."

She kept her word and after dinner, when she stood with Philip on the veranda of the hotel, she had exchanged the way of a child for one of womanly charm. The day was glorious, and already Gay Lewis and the Tilton-Joneses were on hand. A moment later the host of the afternoon led his party to the waiting car. The three ladies occupied the tonneau, while Tilton-Jones and Philip faced them. The New York publisher sat in front with the chauffeur. At the outset Gay Lewis announced her satisfaction. "Nothing could be as fine as this!" she declared. "A Pierce Arrow is next to flying. Of course, for some time to come I shall not be permitted to shoot upward, but if it were not for mother I should accept my first invitation."

"Could you really dare to board an airship?" Mrs. Tilton-Jones put in.

"Certainly," said Gay. "I dare say I was born only for sport; I love it better than anything else in the world. I never think of danger when I am amusing myself."

"I am sorry that we cannot enjoy the afternoon according to latest ideals," the host answered. "However, I must depend upon Miss Lewis to direct our course. Which way shall we take?" he asked.

They had already started on a trip through the little city.

"I am greatly flattered," Gay replied. "But really, I have no choice when I am in a machine. It is just go, go, go, with me. I can almost arrive at Kipling's meter as I sit! sit! sit! bobbing up and down again." Every one laughed.

"And you don't mind a rough road?" Mrs. Tilton-Jones demanded with literal surprise.

"Not as much as most people," Miss Lewis answered. "I, for one, shall not complain this afternoon. I never felt a more comfortable car."

"It moves along perfectly," said Isabel, who had thus far been quiet.

"And will no one dictate our way?" the host again inquired. As he spoke, the chauffeur shot onward in the direction of the mission. Philip alone felt the significance of the driver's plan. But he made up his mind, once and for all, that nothing imaginary should disturb his peace of mind, or ever again come as a phantom between himself and Isabel. He no longer seemed to shrink from a farewell view of the old church. This would be the last one. Nor was he perturbed when later the machine stopped on the verge of the broad pavement leading to steps beyond. Not until Mrs. Tilton-Jones cried out, begging to peep within the mission now resounding with voices of singing monks, did he fully understand. Then he knew, knew that to refuse to go inside on account of afternoon service was to virtually acknowledge himself a disgraced man. In an instant he decided. His wife hesitated, but he insisted that she should get out of the car. Everything happened quickly. With all pressing forward, Philip began to climb the stone flight to the church. There was no escape, he must act as a man. Isabel felt his arm beneath her own. She did not speak. Gay Lewis walked on the other side, and Mrs. Tilton-Jones now joined the row.

"What terrible steps," the lady complained. "I'm not a Catholic, so don't appreciate a penance. But I am delighted to have a look inside. The monks sing wonderfully! just hear them." She chattered on, to the very door. Evidently she had not heard of Philip's former career. Isabel was relieved and entered the church with a sense of unexpected pleasure. She thought she detected the baritone of the brother whom she had once heard; then the voice stilled. A priest was intoning.

Now all Catholics were devoutly kneeling, murmuring evening prayers. Philip Barry stood beside Isabel, with his head slightly bowed. Others of the party used casual time for glancing about the mission. To the man who had once been a priest the voice of the officiating father, the supplicating swell of confessions born of human transgression, the impalpable impression of detached souls coming back to worship, were realities all too startling. Philip had overestimated his strength. He lifted his eyes and saw beyond—far down the long aisle—tall, lighted candles on the holy altar. In brass vases he discerned stalks of flaming poinsettias. Like blood, splashed against the dorsal, the scarlet flowers flanked the golden treasury of the hidden Host. The man had been too long a Catholic to forget. But prayers were over. The choir of brown-hooded monks had burst into praise and ushers peered here and there for vacant sittings. Then, with dismay, the excommunicated priest followed his friends and Isabel the entire length of the old church, to a pew directly in front of the chancel.

He had not counted on the conspicuous placing of a noticeable party. He leaned forward with his head in his hands. Instinctively the usual petition moved his lips. But he sat up and gazed before him with blinding realization of his own false attitude. Why had he entered? Again he recalled honest worshippers of the morning, going up worn stones to early service, at length coming forth into sunlight, with rapt or tranquil faces. And about him were the same reverential men and women. Philip Barry's religious feeling had always been emotional rather than spiritual; still he had been born a Catholic. The beauty of impressive ritualism, the mysticism of the "Elevated Cup," moved his esthetic nature. Dreamer that he was, he knew again the power of his inculcated early training. He thought of his mother. Until to-day every tense effort to recall her sympathetic soul had been vain. Now an impalpable presence reproached him—separated him, as it were, from Isabel. In a momentary vision he saw the dear face and form of his lost one. To his imaginative mind, beautiful old hands stretched out to save him from impending disaster; then everything before his eyes became clear, and he sat still, at the foot of the chancel, a condemned man. Something whispered that to be an outcast from his Church would gradually starve his soul. Perhaps he should turn to stone, forget the worth of Isabel's priceless love and devotion—what then? He shuddered at the thought of possible suffering for his wife. Again the congregation knelt. Again he was glad to bow his head. For the first time since his marriage the dread of disappointing Isabel gripped him. That he should have an insatiate longing for something outside of their close relation filled him with terror. No, she must never know. He stood up at the end of familiar prayers, responding silently to the rich voices above in the choir. At the back of the church the monks had begun a Gloria. After all he would be able to control himself. Then suddenly there was mysterious agitation, moving to and fro of priests and officiating brothers. To visiting Protestants the commotion in the chancel was not appalling. Monks passing hither and thither, priests turning splendid vestments to front and back, seemed but part of an impressive service.

For Philip Barry, duly educated to Catholic power, aware of a ruling order's justified opportunity, there was a plain conclusion. He stood as one summoned, unable to move, waiting for sentence enjoined by his own unpardonable presumption. And above floated the Gloria. Intent on the music Isabel did not turn, did not see Philip's livid face as he stood on, powerless to leave the church, yet knowing the full penalty of remaining. Voices of singing monks withheld judgment. Then finally with the deep Amen a solemn file of officiating brothers marched from the sanctuary. The time had come. Still Philip Barry could not move. Priests turned from the holy altar with plain intent, beginning to disrobe. In stately shame each placed his golden vestment upon a bench. Clad in their cassocks, all went out, save the avenger of the awful hour, now in authority. Philip saw him signal as he came slowly forward to the verge of the chancel. Behind the communion rail he stopped and raised a restraining hand. Above in the choir loft the organ was dumb, not a murmur broke a frightful stillness. The lone priest waited. Every ear strained with his first deliberate utterance. He was looking straight at Philip Barry. At last, he spoke:

"Owing to the presence in this sacred mission of an excommunicated priest, the service is at an end, the congregation is dismissed. Let it go out at once, with downcast eyes and prayers upon the lips of all true Catholics." He walked to the altar and extinguished the last candle, scarcely turning as he drifted from sight of the awe-stricken crowd. The dazed man, singled out for disgrace, stooped to the floor for his hat, rose again to his full imperious height, smiling piteously at Isabel—then he fell backward, caught in the arms of his friend.

Chapter 27

Philip and Isabel were now at home. But the wife had not been able to turn her husband's mind from his late public humiliation. She was frightened, miserable. Would Philip always be as now—crushed, silent with the one he loved best? She buried her face in her hands. Her cheeks burned, while her eyes remained dry. She dared not weep, dared not break down before the changed, listless man whom she would save at any cost to her own anguish. As first days of home-coming dragged away she began to see that she had been presumptuous. After all, her marriage was not to be a happy one. She knew that Philip adored her even more than before the fatal afternoon at the mission, when he had fallen unconscious at her side; yet something obstinate and heart-rending had come between them. Tragic doubt seemed to be freezing her husband's tenderness. With passionate dread of misjudging him she withheld from day to day the question she could not ask. She felt that above all she must wait until the shock of his cruel punishment had ceased to be vivid. During sleepless nights, when she knew for the first time the price of a Catholic priest's apostasy, there came also the realization of personal, unjust punishment. Nor did she acknowledge wrong for either Philip or herself; they had done no wrong. They were created for each other, and their only mistake had been the last imprudent visit to a forbidden place. She grieved over her own ignorance which had permitted Philip to incur the risk which had turned against him. She was bitter, and because of a defensive attitude she could not understand her husband's crushed condition. The joy of those first two weeks at St. Barnabas had departed. Isabel knew that she was a constant reproach to the stricken man, utterly changed and gently silent. Through days when she tried to distract his mind from a forbidden subject, driving him, herself, about the country growing more lovely with each hour of spring, she felt the mutual strain to be almost intolerable. Lurid newspaper accounts of Philip's disgrace had helped to convert their once happy drives into perfunctory, humble attempts to escape notice. Now they went alone in a runabout, avoiding every evidence of ostentation. Country roads lured them from town and led them on to unfrequented foothill slopes, where blue buckthorn adorned sweet-smelling upland acres. Below the purple range deepened with March shadows, swept by fickle sunlight playing over crags and into canyons, the couple passed long intervals when neither one of them spoke. Heart-breaking reticence tied their tongues. Each guessed the thoughts of the other.

All about was the bewildering call of fresh life, yet they could not respond to Nature's glad outburst. Deciduous orchards, flushing buds, early almond blossoms pure as snow, wild flowers, buckthorn, edging miles of stony wash with tender blue, seemed only to evoke prolonged silence. The beauty of everything hurt them, for they were both unhappy and afraid to speak plainly. Then at night, when each lay wide awake, blessing darkness which at last hid their faces, relaxing after false smiles and feigned composure, everything had to be thought out once more. What would come of it all? Philip Barry's wife dared not press the question. She was young and she could not give up easily her dream of love. A passionate undercurrent of hope still helped her to endure the tense situation. Trivialities of everyday life assisted her in deceiving her household. She was gentle with her boy and thoughtful for old madame. Servants saw no change in their mistress. A battle had begun, and, believing in the odds of destiny, Isabel marshalled reserve force and smiled before her little world. But at heart she was frightened. Again and again she remembered the awful moment when she had believed her husband to be dead. Now she imagined the sweeter side of a withheld tragedy. For would Philip forget? Ever be the same man he had been before he went down disgraced in the eyes of a frightened throng fleeing from evil influence? Only a few Protestants understood; but these had come to the rescue, bearing the prostrate stranger into open air—out of the dreadful place. Isabel followed silently behind, like a widow, giving up her dead. When they laid her husband down on the worn stone platform before the mission, she had begged piteously not to halt an instant. But a doctor stayed her anguish with the assurance of Philip's beating heart; and she had dropped unbelieving to his side. Every one had been kind—very kind. But it seemed hours, while she waited—waited! And at last they told her that Philip had only fainted. All that followed was still fresh in her mind. And now as days passed she found it impossible to forget vivid details of the quick departure from St. Barnabas, of a miserable, unexpected home-coming.

Now her main hope was her husband's book: that might save him, yet raise his self-respect to normal. She awaited eagerly a letter of acceptance. To watch for it without appearing to do so was difficult. Once she had missed the postman. Still undoubtedly she would have heard in the event of good news, and good news was sure! To-day, something seemed to cheer her, in spite of Philip's depression. Perhaps it was spring, glorious spring! March had come in as a veritable lamb, and after balmy days Isabel dreaded lowering clouds and rain. As long as she could drive Philip over the country time must appear to pass naturally, while in temporary confinement it would be harder to keep up pretenses. Already what is known in California as a "weather breeder" seemed to overcharge the senses, and even as Isabel left the foothills for the the homeward down-grade spin she felt a change. By early evening clouds were forming above the mountains; next day the sun refused to shine, and by night it rained so hard that March took on an Eastern temper and announced a storm. Isabel was disturbed at the prospect of seclusion. Once she had loved rain as well as sunshine, but now she listened to the incessant downpour with sinking heart. If only the publisher's letter would come. She realized anew her husband's strange condition, which instead of lifting was getting worse. Despondency was gnawing at his self-respect. He was ill, shattered beyond his own control. And his wife felt powerless to call a physician. For Philip had been obdurate with their home-coming, had refused to consult a doctor. Isabel feared to press the matter, yet wondered if she were wise to wait. Perhaps Philip's sudden fall had been more than mere fainting! The shock of public dishonor might have broken a blood vessel of his brain—a vessel so tiny that consciousness had soon returned. She told herself that at the end of the storm she would unburden her full story to a reliable specialist, then bring him to see her husband. She could no longer endure the strain alone. The determination brought her comfort, while with the force of her definite will she began to plan for intervening hours of rain. First of all, the open fire of the living-room should not die down a moment. Like a vestal watching her lamp, she piled on wood until the dark paneled walls reflected the glow of a rising blaze. Then she enticed Philip and Reginald and madame about the hearth. Cheer within made compelling contrast to a dreary outside. And all day long she strove to divert her husband's mind from desperate musing. Madame read in French, or the boy manipulated toy automobiles between the rugs; and when these things failed, the latest liveliest music was run off on a really fine mechanical piano which until now had been practically forgotten. By early bedtime the strenuous day seemed an improvement on previous ones with pensive opportunity in the open. Isabel was hopeful, glad to believe that Philip would sleep. She felt weary herself, and sank to rest without the usual effort of nights past, and rain fell on.

Chapter 28

Very early in the morning a cloud burst flooded the valley. Little rivers ran on thoroughfares, and town gutters widened into dashing streams. Isabel awakened with a start, to hear the water in the Arroyo Seco roaring like some mad thing released. Rampant, swollen, an oncoming charge from the mountains struck a stony vent, transforming a dry, volcanic bed into a running torrent. At intervals lightning flashed lurid sheets, with distant rumbling thunder. The storm had broken into alarming fury.

"Are you awake?" asked Isabel, knowing too well that Philip was not sleeping.

"Yes," he confessed. "Shall I get up and look after the windows?"

She knew that he was trying to appear thoughtful. She assured him that every part of the house had been made secure before retiring. The two lay still, listening to the tempest.

"Isn't it frightful?" Isabel said timidly.

"I like it," her husband answered.

The wail of the storm seemed a dirge to pent thoughts. Philip offered no tenderness to allay her fear, and she was afraid. Suddenly there came a rush of wind and a blasting zigzag charge, with terrible instantaneous crashing thunder. The clap reverberated unchained through the mountains. In a second of powerful light Isabel forgot personal terror, forgot everything but Philip's face. For at last she knew the truth; saw the unchecked anguish of his tortured soul. It was all worse than she had thought. He was ill—very ill. Her arms went out about his neck. Her stored up tears fell free against his cheek. Isabel's self-control was lost. She could no longer, hide her fear. She had waited patiently, she would speak!

"Tell me! oh tell me!" she implored. "I cannot bear it—I shall die if you do not tell me." The secret she had caught gave her fierce strength. "You wish to leave me, you are sorry! You want to go away because you think it is a sin to love me? You are miserable because you gave up—left your Church?" Everything was bursting from her like the tempest. "I could let you go," she sobbed, "but I cannot believe that we have done wrong. It is too cruel. I cannot give you up. Your God never meant you to suffer alone. If you go back they will make you suffer—never let you forget. And—and you could not forget that I am your wife—that you love me?"

She clung to him in fear. Would he answer her—deny what she said? "You do love me?" she softened at the thought, and kissed his forehead. "We love each other as God meant we should. We will blot out the past, live! You shall be another man." She was pleading her own case with Philip's. Her tears had ceased to fall. "We will do good jointly, do something to better the world, a world outside of narrow creeds and inhuman dogma." She would not acknowledge the advantage of his lost opportunity. Individual power for accomplishment was as honorable as to bow beneath a yoke. Her argument had been forming through miserable days. "Life is beautiful! most beautiful when we may help others to enjoy it. When your book comes out——"

Philip sprang up, tearing loose her arms. Then he fell back. She thought again that he was dead. She tried to turn on light and failed. Something had been struck in the garden! The terrific bolt must have severed main electric wires. Trembling in darkness she thought of a wax taper on the dressing table and felt about for matches. In a momentary flash through the window she found what she sought. But she dreaded to look at Philip. What if—she approached the bed, then he sat up and spoke to her as one utterly despairing.

"Never speak of the book again," he implored. He sank on the pillow, and she waited for him to go on. "I should have told you—forgive me," he said at last. "The manuscript has come back."

Isabel burst into fresh tears. She seemed powerless to remember her husband's alarming condition. "No! no!" she sobbed. "You cannot mean it,—there is some mistake. The book will make you famous, it cannot fail!"

"But it has failed," he answered with momentary strength. "They do not care to publish it; it stands dishonored like—the man who wrote it."

She blanched at his words. "Come back! Your manuscript returned?" she faltered. "You cannot mean it; where is the letter? I must see it."

He smiled piteously, pointing to a closed desk at the other side of the room, where she found the pasteboard box loosely held in brown paper. The name of a prominent publishing house was stamped outside the wrapper and inside was the letter.

She read, re-read, with burning cheeks—a polite, commercial decision; then she ran to Philip. Her eyes were blazing with champion light; her courage had returned. Great love for the stricken man gone down before a flood of disappointment enveloped her being. The force of her wonderful nature rose up for fresh battle.

"Darling!" she pleaded, "you are too ill to understand." She caught his hand as she crept close to his side. "They like your book,—know that it is fine; but they are afraid of the cost of publishing it. The pictures have frightened them and they are too commercial to take the risk of a sumptuous volume. One refusal is nothing! Our new friend will know the value of your work, and the manuscript must go to him at once." The positive current of her magnetic will, the plausibility of her conviction, above all, her tenderness, seemed a divine anodyne for Philip's sinking soul. Yet he dared not hope. The shaft of disgrace had been sunk too straight. He was too ill to resist remorse; too weak to deny the penalty for broken vows; too hopeless to defy authority which had thrust him down and trodden upon his self-respect. On the verge of fatal prostration, no sins were blacker than his own. Darkest of all appeared a selfish love forced upon innocent Isabel. Dishonored man that he was, she must share his shame. He closed his weary eyes.

His wife clung to his hand. But one thought possessed her,—to call a nerve specialist. Time had passed for deliberation, now she would act.

"Darling," she whispered, "I am going to send for a doctor." He protested, and she went on softly, pleading her right. "You will not stop me this time, as you did when first we came home? You are not well. I cannot bear to see you growing worse when I might bring relief." She felt him bending to her stronger nature, and with streaks of day showing through an atmosphere of mist, her will power seemed to be restored.

He was so quiet that she believed him to be sleeping. She dared not move, still holding his hand, thinking of all which morning might bring forth. That unreasonable dread of life was beginning to threaten Philip's reason, she did not know; nor could she understand the condition of a person trained to religious conformity, then suddenly cast adrift, without spiritual sounding line. It had not occurred to her to doubt her husband's power to live on contentedly without settled, sectarian belief. A religious education had not entered into her own childhood, and as she grew older she formulated views and ethical standards which could not be called orthodox. Her mind had developed independently.

What an apostate priest might suffer she could not readily divine. That Philip had been born with power to move his fellowmen through spoken thoughts she did not seriously consider; nor did she understand that a vital preacher is distinct in his calling. As she lay with closed eyes—yet wide awake—she built only on the wisdom of a specialist who should—who must—help her.

Then suddenly Philip spoke.

"Yes, dear," she answered. "I thought you were sleeping."

"Don't send for a doctor," he pleaded. "Let me rest—just here—I will soon be better." His face touched her own and she felt that his eyes were moist. A tear rolled down between their cheeks.

Chapter 29

A lull following the tempest seemed an anodyne for broken rest. Philip forgot his anguish through exhaustion, while Isabel dropped into slumber, which always restored her power to hope. Perfect health sustained her. She clung to the determination to hold her dearly bought happiness despite discouraging odds. At broad daylight she lay awake and watchful by the side of her husband. Through open casements the wet sweetness of the morning recharged her nerves. Birds twittered excitedly from drenched trees. The nearby arroyo sent outward a song of drops, piling over stones. Isabel recalled a time when she had been awakened by the musical splash of Roman fountains. Then, as now, Philip Barry claimed her thoughts, set them bounding to the irresistible measure of falling water. During those days she had listened to the rhythmic call in the old palace garden, only to wonder about Philip and the possible outcome of their fresh young love. It seemed a long way back since those ideal weeks. This morning as she lay still and anxious her mind began to revert to incidental happenings which had parted a boy and a girl, but to join them later under tense conditions. She turned with caution and peered into Philip's face. His secret had touched his countenance with unconscious despair. His cheeks were growing hollow. Around his compressed mouth Isabel saw deepening lines. She felt again that her husband could be saved only with the help of a discerning specialist. Time seemed precious and she slipped softly from the sleeper's side to her own room. It was early for a bath, but her firm young flesh cried out for refreshment as she plunged into cool water. Strength came as the result of a regular habit and she dressed quickly, then went below. Only Wing, the Chinese cook, was at his post. Maids, kept awake by the storm, had overslept. Isabel wandered through a closed house to find her faithful celestial already at work. His white garments, noiseless shoes, and optimistic smile always gave her pleasure. "Good morning," she said.

Wing turned in evident dismay. "Why you up so early?" he asked with the childlike freedom of the Oriental. "Those girls heap lazy! not come down yet—house all dark." He spread his slender brown hands in feigned disgust. "I gless you not know that big tree fall over las night? Most hit my klitchen. You come see." He threw open the screen, pointing beyond. Isabel saw a Monterey pine low and done for by the storm. Heavy, drenched branches, crushed and aromatic, rose from the ground to the top of a nearby porch, which had just escaped them. Years of growth and vigor were down with a blast from the surcharged sky. She seemed to feel the human significance of the fallen pine.

"Poor thing!" she exclaimed, peering into upturned limbs of the vanquished tree. "Poor thing!"

Wing beamed. His white teeth flashed credulous interest. "You think that tree get hurt—all same me?" he demanded. Isabel saw that she was planting fresh superstition on celestial soil.

"I am not quite sure," she answered. "Still, a great tree could hardly tear away from earth without feeling it. It must have suffered," she maintained. Unconsciously she was thinking of her husband. That Philip had been uprooted, cast down like the pine filled her with dread as she went quickly from the kitchen. But the storm, which left the house in total darkness during the night had also interfered with telephone service. After vain attempts to communicate with the central office, she dashed off a note to a well-known nerve specialist. She begged him to come at once, explaining that her husband was too ill to leave his bed. From the terrace she watched the gardener depart with her note. She felt at last like one who stakes all on a final venture. Would the doctor come soon? Would Philip resent the visit? Above all, how should she break the news to the invalid, who begged to be left alone? "Don't call a doctor," he had pleaded; and again she wondered if she had been wise in a grave emergency. The house was now astir. Belated maids were at work. Soon shrill exclamations arose from the wet garden. Madame had discovered the fallen pine, to fly below with the boy. Reginald was proudly equipped with rubber boots. His red coat flashed as he outran his excited companion. Isabel translated the French woman's lament for the lost tree; then the boy cried out in distress. His mother reached his side to find him in tears, holding a dead oriole. The once gay, golden little creature lay limp in the child's hand.

"Poor birdy! See, he's all, all broken!" he bemoaned. "Can't you mend him, mother dear? Can't you make him stand up?"

"He has been hurt by the storm," Isabel explained, stroking the feathers of the little victim. "Perhaps he lived in the pine tree. We may find his nest."

Reginald began to search along the path, while Isabel found a sharpened stick. When she came to a clump of ferns she bent and quickly dug a tiny bed in the wet earth. Her son, running back, saw that the oriole was gone.

"There wasn't any nest!" he shouted, gazing incredulously at his mother's empty hand, "And I suppose the poor birdy's all mended. Why didn't you wait? I wanted—I wanted to see him fly away." Fresh tears betokened the boy's disappointment. Isabel felt justified in the deception, as she led the child indoors. He would understand soon enough.

Wing had just brought back a dainty tray, with everything on it declined by the master. The good fellow was greatly distressed. "Boss not eat—he die! Sure!" he muttered.

Isabel went above. She felt again that she had done right in calling a physician, and strove for courage to announce the approaching visit. When she entered her husband's room he seemed to be dozing. She did not rouse him. Perhaps, after all, sleep would prove to be Philip's best medicine, and something whispered that her apparent anxiety was not good for the broken man she loved. She went out, acknowledging a mistake. When Philip awoke she would tell him about the doctor, with incidental lightness. Then sooner than she expected she heard an automobile and knew that her note had been timely. The specialist was at hand—in the hall below. She could not prepare Philip for an unwelcome call. But she was eager to unburden her heart, willing to rest her fear with one who ought to assume it. And at once she told of her husband's early education, of the first success of his priesthood, of his ambition for a great Middle West cathedral, of the bishop's unjust course, of Philip's natural struggle, followed with excommunication from the Church; then all too soon—before he could readjust his life—of the public humiliation in the old mission. She kept nothing back but her own hard part as the wife of an apostate priest. The dread that she had been the sole cause of a brilliant man's undoing she bravely acknowledged. Philip could not forget, could not supplement his relinquished work with domestic happiness.

"Yet he adores me," she confessed. "It is not just that he should suffer—as he does. His heart is breaking. He feels it a sin to love me—to go on with happiness."

"And you?" said Dr. Judkin.

She tried to smile. "Women can bear more than men." Her voice broke.

The man by her side felt her charm, knew that she was valiant in love. Still he saw disappointment in her tense resistance. "I am afraid that you, too, will soon need attention," he abruptly told her. "Sometimes a wife spoils her husband without realizing it. Men who think a great deal about themselves are not considerate."

She was offended and replied coldly, "You do not know him. It is unjust to judge of a patient before you have seen him."

"I stand reproved," the doctor admitted.

Isabel forgave him. His very bluntness brought her hope. Suddenly she felt faith in the man whom she had summoned. She believed that he was masterful, and she must turn to some one.

"Please come," she invited, "you shall see my husband."

Dr. Judkin stood aside for her to pass, and she went above, choosing words which should explain his early call. Then at the top of the staircase she stopped.

"Be good enough to wait," she begged. "I must prepare him—go in first." Then she flew forward, for the smell of burning paper had caught her nostrils. The door to Philip's apartment was fastened. She had been locked out! She rushed to a balcony running before the windows of her husband's room. In an instant she stood within. And she had not come a moment too soon. A fresh tragedy faced her. She hardly breathed. Philip, on his knees in front of the fireplace, did not hear her enter. The ecstasy of delirium possessed him. His whole body trembled as he showered an igniting pile with his rejected manuscript. "The Spirit of the Cathedral" was smoking. Isabel saw rising flame desert a blackened sketch of a famous duomo but to lick a painting of great St. Peter's. Once more dominant Romish power appeared to threaten. The curse of the Church seemed about to blaze anew for Philip.

Her heart thumped as she flew to his side. "How can you?" she pleaded. "You have forgotten your friend—who trusted you. You must not spoil his beautiful pictures." Her hand reached out and coolly rescued scorching sheets of the unpublished book. "But you did not mean to hurt an artist's work," she gently added. She held a ruined sketch before the sick man's staring eyes. "You did not remember. You did not mean to be unfair to your friend." The tenderness of her frightened, loving soul broke over the shattered man, as she led him away to bed. He went like an obedient child; then she unlocked the door and summoned the doctor.

Chapter 30

Two trained nurses had been installed. Isabel no longer held her place at Philip's bedside. She was virtually banished from her husband's room. The courage which she had evinced during previous weeks seemed to be going fast. Now she hardly dared to hope. A silent house already took on the atmosphere of disaster. Even Reginald was not permitted to shout in the garden. And withal spring was at hand, seemingly to brighten the whole world, outside of Philip's closed apartments. The sap of fresh life ran in the veins of every living thing in the valley, on the foothills, above in the mountains. The season had advanced without a check, while throughout the Southwest blooming fruit trees and millions of roses prepared the land for Easter.

To Isabel sensuous beauty on every side seemed cruel. Her heart felt desolate. She went through each day wishing for night, while with darkness she longed for sunlight. Suspense was beginning to drain her vitality. She did not complain, but the doctor saw her brace herself against each discouraging outcome of days that dragged. For Philip's last collapse had turned her from his side. She was barely a memory to the man she loved. At first she had rebelled, then accepted conditions enjoined by Dr. Judkin and consulting specialists. Only one thing helped her to endure the strain of a cruel separation.

Philip's book—now speaking to her heart as she knew it would speak—brought strange, proud comfort. She felt exalted that she—his wife—had saved the manuscript from the flames. During a week she fairly lived in the scorched pages of "The Spirit of the Cathedral." And gradually she began to see why the work had been refused. Personal feeling and blind enthusiasm were at last tempered. She could read with a cool intellect. The Laodicean attitude of a shrewd publisher hurt her less than at first. For the fact still remained that Philip had produced something fine. Although he occasionally dropped his impassioned theme to give vent to slight discord, nothing had really been lost from his original motif. Reading between the lines, Isabel detected the natural temptation under which he had worked. Certain paragraphs, all unaided by a magnetic voice and delivery, read too much like his former sermons. Sometimes overcharged, almost vindictive handling of Romish background was evident. In those first weeks in Paris, after he had deserted the priesthood and been cast out of the Church, he had written without restraint. He had said things best left unsaid. Yet, as Isabel read on, she marvelled at Philip's virile touch, at the masterful, dramatic power of his pen. His word pictures drawn from vivid, exceptional opportunity required no literal illustration. Still she studied the sketches of the associate artist, finally selecting one fourth of the cathedrals submitted. Then she read over again the stronger chapters of the singed manuscript. It was late into night before she weighed the possible chances of her husband's book. He had labored so intelligently that her hand seemed to be guided by his own as she omitted paragraphs which undoubtedly influenced the publishers to refuse a somewhat prejudiced work.

Isabel felt free to decide for Philip. His extremity excused her arbitrary action. She was sure that in his normal condition he would agree to all that she had done. When scorched pages had been replaced by fresh ones she would send the revised manuscript to the publisher she had met at St. Barnabas, the one who had witnessed the withstayed tragedy in the mission. She believed that her new friend could appreciate the significance of a book written by one who not only criticised expertly, but knew as well the human side of a great cathedral. Her thoughts went back to a time when Philip—a priest—had outlined plans for the noble church he hoped to build. Then nothing seemed too big for his young city. Isabel smiled, and began to read once more.

Suddenly tears came to her eyes. She put aside the manuscript. After all, what right had she to tamper with her husband's work? From Philip's higher standpoint, painted or stone saints and angels, looking down from Gothic heights, meant nothing to her, outside of their mere artistic value. She saw with fresh dread that Philip was still a Catholic. Early education and his lost mother's devout influence kept him apart from natural happiness. He should have remained a priest, a power in his Church. She remembered how once she had stood with him in St. Peter's—in front of the "Pieta." He had then almost forgotten her presence. The wrapt significance of his expression ought to have warned her. She felt once more that she would never be able to share her husband's feeling for an old master's sacred ideal. And later, when the two were passing the noted bronze of St. Peter, she recalled that she had failed to hide her repulsion for the throng straining to kiss the statue's jutting, shining toe. Philip divined her thoughts and flushed. "It comforts them," he had whispered. "Over here the poor have so little in their lives. What seems absurd to you is for them salvation."

To-night Isabel remembered everything now bearing on her husband's tragic state. Her heart grew heavy with fear, with vague foreboding.

Chapter 31

Philip's physical condition had improved during six weeks of masterful nursing. Isabel was at last permitted to see him for ten short minutes; then she kept her promise and went from the room. This morning she sank into a chair, mutely listening to the doctor's voice.

"He has come out much better than I expected," he confessed. "Our nurses have left nothing undone. The patient has responded to the limit of his burned-down condition. We shall save him."

She lifted a face wet with tears. "Oh," she begged, "may I help—do some little thing? I have waited so long. It has been hard, hard, to see other women always at his side, when his wife might not even give him a glass of water."

Rebellion which she had hidden through past days burst forth. "May I not let one of the nurses go? I long to do my natural part."

Dr. Judkin stopped pacing. "Listen to me," he commanded. She braced herself for fresh disappointment, knowing well the superior wisdom of the man's despotic practice. "Listen!" he repeated. "You have already done what few women can do—submitted magnificently to a passive part. And you have helped me more than you will ever know." She felt a new demand back of his words. "Now is the crucial test of your will power. I have been waiting anxiously for this particular point in your husband's case. The physical collapse has been arrested and he is now ready for a complete change of scene. He needs a sea voyage, with continued quiet, but nothing familiar to arouse consciousness of past events."

"Oh," she cried, "I may take him abroad? Perhaps to Japan? I can go to any part of the world which you think best for him." Her voice rang joy. Color ran into her cheeks. "You have been so good to me—so patient with my own impatience. And I knew that you could save him! Something told me that first awful morning that you would help me, that you would be my friend."

The doctor stood powerless to tell her his real decision. Through weeks he had felt the passionate suffering beneath her well-bred composure. Character had stilled her bursting heart. He frowned, looking down at a pattern in the rug.

"You have not quite understood me," he said at last. "The change of which I speak must be absolute, entirely outside of—of—tempting association. As yet the patient must sink reviving interest in life to the dead level of his nurse, to the advent of meals served on the deck of a quiet ship."

"You mean that I should engage a private yacht?" Isabel eagerly asked. "I know of one owned by a friend who will let me have it. Shall I wire at once?"

Again the man by her side was baffled. Of late his brusque announcements had perceptibly softened. To-day, knowing as only a physician does, the tragedy of certain marital relations, this woman's great love rebuked his ruthless plan. Still he must speak, make a professional edict clear. "But you are not to accompany your husband," he abruptly told her. "You might undo the work of weeks, make the patient's ultimate recovery doubtful."

His words came hard, plain. Isabel sat stunned and silent.

"Philip Barry will come back from his voyage another man," the doctor deliberately promised. "And the separation will not be as hard as it now seems. After the fight for your husband's life and reason you may feel that we are about to conquer. Tahiti—the isle of rest—will restore him wholly."

Isabel did not answer. Only tightly clasped hands betrayed her agitation. The doctor went on:

"I have taken the voyage to Tahiti myself. Five years ago I was a nervous wreck when I sailed from San Francisco. Twenty-one days later, when I landed at the Society Islands, at Tahiti, I was a new man. Weeks on the water, without a word from the world behind me had worked a miracle. On the upper deck of the comfortable little ship I forgot my troubles through pure joy of existence. All day long I rested body and brain. With evening the blood-red sun plunged into a molten sea. Then blue sky suddenly changed to violet, and deepening shadow brought out the stars—the Southern Cross. I began to feel like a different person."

An eloquent outburst awakened no response. The doctor saw that he must speak decidedly. His next words fell with brutal authority.

"Your husband must be made ready to start for San Francisco at once. A boat leaves Port Los Angeles day after to-morrow. It is best that our patient should avoid the train, and in going by water he will have half a day and a night to rest in some good hotel. The ship sails at noon,—on the seventeenth."

He was beginning to think that Mrs. Barry's silence meant compliance. Resignation seemed to be a part of her marvelous character.

And at last she unclasped her hands, pressing them before her eyes. But he heard her gently sobbing.

"Don't!" he humbly entreated. "You must not forget what I have promised. You shall have your husband back—well! He will put all behind him! forget everything but his wife."

She did not answer. Dr. Judkin waited until her hands left her eyes. Then she began to speak with fresh determination.

"Why can I not go too? on the same boat, just to be near him in case he needs me. I should not let him know that I was on board, not make even a sign,—unless—he missed me. Oh! let me go with him. It is not fair that another woman should have my place—my absolute right to be near him. He is my husband! I cannot bear it."

Tempered passion could no longer conceal her feeling. She was blazing with jealous rebellion. For the time being the nurse who had given satisfaction was an enemy—a woman usurping the place of Philip's wife. Yet the specialist knew that she would submit. She loved too perfectly to withstand reason. Suddenly he saw his way out of a tense situation.

"I had forgotten to tell you," he interrupted, "I am going to send my assistant, Dr. Ward. Our patient is so much better that it seems to be time for an absolute change, even in regard to his nurse. When Philip Barry returns he will be another man. Dr. Ward is the best of company, a splendid fellow, with rare common sense." He saw her tremble. "We will engage a special ship steward to assist, and everything shall be done for your husband's comfort."

Her face lifted like a smitten flower. The blaze in her eyes subsided. She looked into the doctor's face as a conquered child. "I have been very weak—very unreasonable," she faltered. "Now I will do everything that you think best,—make you no more trouble." She tried to laugh. "I am going to be good,—good like Reg."

"Then we shall get out of the woods," he answered. "And mind—you are not to grow thin while Philip Barry grows fat in Tahiti. If you are really going to be good you must relax, put away anxiety. When Philip comes home he must see you in the height of bloom. I first want you to go to bed at least for a week. Then you may take to the saddle, cultivate friends, enjoy yourself as every one should in God's country—in springtime."

To-day Dr. Judkin seemed pleased with the world. His patient was more than promising, while Mrs. Barry appealed to him irresistibly. He put out his hand, doggedly determined to save her husband. "Keep a brave heart," he prescribed, "everything is now going our way."

But once outside he asked himself if courage such as Isabel's deserved the test of possible disappointment. What, after all, must be the outcome of Philip Barry's recovery? Would he realize fresh obligation to a woman's almost divine love? Would he be able to put out of his own life withering emotions of regret? Dr. Judkin had not known his patient before the total collapse of weeks back, and he could not consistently answer hard questions. To vouch for the man's future behavior was, after all, impossible; and yet, he had just promised Isabel to save him for years to come. The futility of finite judgment, the mistakes of theoretical practice, the guesswork involved in a case such as Barry's, tempered the specialist's confidence. He went flying on his way depressed. Then he remembered that Isabel seemed to be an absolute exception to many of the wives belonging to her apparently enviable station. She gave out for joy of giving. Love such as hers refused to be measured by modern standards or a husband's limitations.

Chapter 32

Isabel was parted from Philip. She had watched him sail from Port Los Angeles, then quickly entered a waiting touring car. Dr. Judkin's fears were groundless, as the homeward trip had proved to be pleasant, almost like a vent for the wife's tense feeling. It was clear that she had staked everything on her husband's ocean voyage. Despite a hard separation she was hopeful. She seemed determined to accept present conditions, meanwhile living for the fulfillment of happier months to come.

And with her usual force, she at once began to engage in active matters. Dr. Judkin's injunction to rest was forgotten. She seemed to be suddenly strong. The doctor's rash promise intoxicated her; Philip, just gone, was dearer than ever. She said over and over that he would come back well, able to respond to fresh opportunities. He should find them waiting, and friends, too. It was yet early in the day. Isabel dressed carefully, ordered her carriage and went forth to pay visits. New acquaintances must see that she was not a crushed wife. She wanted to tell every one that her husband was getting better. The splendid pride of her young nature rose up for conquest. Pity was not for Isabel. And after a pleasant outing she returned to find the house, withal, more cheerful than for weeks back. Nurses had gone, and Reginald's unrestrained shouts echoed at will.

"Mother darling! Mother darling!" the little fellow had cried. "How pretty your dress is! Have you been getting married this afternoon? Please read me a story like you used to," he demanded.

"I will tell you one," Isabel said gently. Then she gathered her son in her arms. His head rested against her breast, as she began to tell him about far-away Tahiti. She colored a simple narrative until it glowed with personal interest. The boy listened happily. A little brown hand held her own fairer one, turning her jeweled rings, while she pictured "Father Philip's" boat, the island in the middle of the ocean, native boys and girls selling garlands, the possibility of whales, of flying fish, and everything else that naturally belonged to the story. With Philip as her hero, Isabel felt able to spin indefinite situations for sea or land. Spring twilight seemed to cast its spell over mother and son. The English nurse came twice before the tale of Tahiti was finished. Reginald, unmindful of a supper of bread and milk, paid no heed to an invitation; and for some new reason Isabel encouraged her boy to disregard hitherto accepted authority.

"When I have eated a lot and get all weddy for bed I'll come back," the little fellow at last promised. "I want some more 'lapping' and another story about the big whales. Then I'll say my French prayer." He hopped away on one leg. Isabel heard his voice piping triumph. "I'm coming back! I'm coming back! Goody! goody! She said I might." Then the door closed.

Isabel sat on, thinking of past silent weeks, asking herself if her boy had not been harshly treated. Dear little chap! he might now make noise. Later the child kept his word, rushing down in night clothes for his good night "lapping," for one more story. After all, time was passing. And to-morrow Philip would be in San Francisco, then by noon of the next day he would sail for Tahiti. Isabel decided once more to keep her mind employed during her husband's absence. Madame pined to play cribbage, and evening was well spent before the two friends bade each other good night. The old French woman had won several rubbers and retired in high spirits, while the younger one went softly to her boy's bedside.

As usual, Reginald lay tucked in his white nest on an upper balcony. A half moon shut out by falling canvas shot beams across a screen of interlacing vines. The sleeping boy was bathed in radiance. His arms rested outside the covers and one little brown hand still held a toy locomotive. Isabel bent and touched her son's soft brow. His relaxed beauty thrilled her. As often before, the boy reminded her of Bellini's sleeping child—the one lying across the Madonna's lap—in the Academy at Venice. She had boldly rebelled that the wonderful picture was unstarred in the great master's collection of holy children. To-night her mother-heart still deplored an arbitrary test of art. She drew aside a curtain, gazing upward to the sky. A star too brilliant for the moon's effacement looked down, while seemingly no erring human judgment could check a heavenly tribute to her sleeping boy. She went from his side strangely happy. But she did not enter Philip's closed room. Rather, she desired to shut out those weeks of torture and anxiety. She thought of Dr. Judkin's rash promise, of the time when her husband would come back well; of his book, which she had fortunately saved from the flames. And it was now time to hear definitely from the manuscript; almost four weeks since it had gone upon its journey eastward. The publisher had written at once, announcing his interest in Philip's work, yet of course the matter could not be decided too hastily. Isabel had waited patiently. Now that she was alone it seemed harder to endure a new kind of suspense. What if the manuscript came back? No! no! that must not happen, not again. She dared not dwell on a crushing possibility and went to bed, driving the thought from her. After all, she would accept Dr. Judkin's advice and take to the saddle. She would ride to-morrow—throughout the bright spring morning. Miss Lewis, who had fortunately returned to town, should use one of the horses. Then perhaps Gay could stop for a short visit—stay until after Philip's boat had sailed. She buried her face in the pillow.

Chapter 33

Miss Lewis was pleased to accept a welcome invitation. Next morning the two friends mounted early for a canter through the valley. Isabel rode her husband's horse, while Gay exulted over the restive temper of Mrs. Barry's more spirited animal.

"You darling!" she cried, when finally she controlled the pretty creature, too keen for a race. Afterward, the thoroughbreds from the foothills went side by side. Miss Lewis was in high spirits. Love of action seemed to be expressed in every line of her trim little figure. Isabel felt the charm of her friend's free grace, and dashed forward with unchecked speed. A long avenue lined with palms, towering eucalyptus trees, and draping peppers reached for miles across the valley dressed for April's carnival. The air was intoxicating. Millions of flowers—roses, climbing, climbing, seemed to blaze a sacrifice to spring. Isabel's heart lightened with the glory of the day. For the time being she forgot that to-morrow was the seventeenth. That Philip was about to enter the Golden Gate, about to spend a few last hours in San Francisco before sailing on his long voyage, fortunately escaped her mind. Quick to understand, Miss Lewis led the way. She dashed onward for an hour, then nearer mountains appeared to turn for a fresh landscape. All at once remote, giant, snowclad peaks became the center of the horizon, lifting from acres of dark-green orange groves, flecked with golden fruit and snowy blossoms. Gay dropped from the saddle, while her horse began to graze by the roadside. Mrs. Barry kept her mount with loosened bridle. They had gone a long distance into the valley. The spell of spring was upon them both.

"It is all too lovely for earth!" cried Gay.

"Too lovely for sorrow and disappointment," Isabel answered. A shadow passed over her face. She was at last thinking of Philip.

Miss Lewis impulsively drew in her horse, springing to her seat like a boy. "Come on," she begged, "I have something else to show you." She stripped off her glove, holding up her hand. "Is it not a beauty?" A black opal surrounded with canary diamonds flashed in sunlight. "I chose the ring myself," she confessed. "I have always been wild over black opals, have always intended to have one when I settled down for life." She laughed and dashed onward.

"Tell me all about him," Isabel called out. "I am so glad that you are happy. I cannot wait,—do tell me."

The horses were now walking side by side. Miss Lewis leaned, shaking, over the pommel of her saddle. "Who said there was a man in the story?" she demanded. "How quickly you arrive at conclusions. Did I not say that I chose the ring myself? But I will tell you." She turned lightly to her friend. "My engagement is another case of 'Marjory Daw.' There isn't any suitor, only a ranch of six hundred acres on which I intend to live the greater part of the year. I am crazy about it! The papers are being prepared and as soon as I have full possession I shall build a bungalow, a barn, and a garage. My black opal simply means that I am engaged to my new estate; that I am going to be the happiest bachelor girl in Southern California." She laughed gaily, starting her horse on a run. "Come on! Come on!" she called.

They dashed miles across the country before they turned for home. Isabel had no opportunity for pensive thoughts. The sun had touched the zenith when the thoroughbreds stood in their stalls. Luncheon waited for two hungry women.

Suddenly a long-distance call summoned Isabel to the telephone. She left the table vaguely conscious of fresh trouble. The receiver trembled in her hand, she could hardly control herself. But soon she was listening in rapture. From far-away San Francisco a familiar voice vibrated over the wire—her husband spoke to her! "Catch the owl—to-night—join me to-morrow—at the dock," he implored. She heard him distinctly, attempted to answer, when the connection broke. Again and again the operator tried to restore the line. Communication with Philip was hopelessly lost. The disappointment seemed more than Isabel could endure, and she buried her face and wept. The voice of the man she loved still rang out in her imagination. She heard him commanding, begging her to come. "I will! I will!" she answered. She seemed almost to be repeating their marriage service. "Dear, dear husband, I am coming. No power on earth shall keep me from you." She laughed softly as she again caught the receiver.

"Give me one, six, double three!" she entreated. She hardly breathed while she waited. A woman's voice said, "Dr. Judkin's office," and Isabel announced herself. "The doctor is occupied with a patient—he cannot be interrupted. Will you please give me your message?" the attendant answered.

"He must come—at once! I cannot wait!" Isabel begged. "Tell him that Mrs. Barry wishes to speak with him; he will understand. I cannot lose a moment. I am going North to join my husband." Her words rang with decision. She no longer trembled and her tears had been dashed away. Her cheeks burned. In the little closet where she tarried an electric bulb blazed no brighter than her eyes. Why did the doctor not come? Why, after all, had she asked for him? Was she not going to Philip at once? There was indeed no time to lose if she packed for a voyage and caught the evening train in Los Angeles for San Francisco. Her heart thumped like a trip-hammer as she sat clutching the receiver, now fairly glued to her ear. And at last she recognized the voice of Dr. Judkin and repeated her previous statement.

"I'm going North to-night—on the Owl—to Philip. He wants me. He has just telephoned a long-distance message. I am to join him to-morrow—at the dock." Her voice fairly danced. "Why do you not answer?" she implored. "You surely understand?"

"My poor, poor child," she heard at last. "Would you ruin all that we have done? You must not go. Emphatically, you must not sail with your husband." The receiver dropped. Her head went forward against her arms crossed on the table. But she could not weep. The luxury of tears was beyond her strength to shed them. When she lifted her head she was in the dark; the electric bulb had burned out. And next day, at the same hour, in the same spot, she first heard of the earthquake, of the total destruction of San Francisco.

Chapter 34

Time dragged for Isabel. Like every one else with friends in the North, she tried in vain to hear directly from San Francisco. Communication had been completely cut off for the ill-fated city; wrecked, now burning above the useless bay. Isabel sat for hours listening and waiting. Still no word from Philip. The sound of his far-away voice, his last request, asking her to come to him, echoed in her brain. She felt that she might lose her reason. All the fine courage of weeks back was gone. Dr. Judkin, Miss Lewis, and old madame, each tried in turn to allay her fear. She could not hope. The only person whose sympathy seemed to be of value was Cole's, for the man from the foothills offered to go North and hunt for Philip. "I'll get into the city some way," he promised. "If Mr. Barry's on land I'll find him." Isabel would have accepted the warm-hearted offer but for Dr. Judkin. "Ten chances to one your husband was on shipboard before the earthquake took place," he stoutly maintained. "I know that Dr. Ward had at first intended spending the night at the St. Francis; then he changed his plan, deciding to get his patient settled as soon as possible in the steamer's cabin. He feared the excitement of the hotel and felt sure that the Tahiti boat would be lying at anchor." Isabel did not reply and he went on. "Suspense is hard to endure, but I rely on you to wait a few days longer, when we are then sure to hear something. While flames are raging in the streets, with dynamite blowing up blocks of buildings, we cannot hope for reliable information. But one thing is certain—Dr. Ward is going to take care of Philip Barry. If the two men are not out at sea they are simply unable to let us know of their safety on account of both martial law and prevailing conditions."

"I should have gone to him when he called me!" Isabel answered. "Then I would have been there—when it happened. Oh, why did you keep me from going?" For the first time Dr. Judkin felt unable to control his patient's wife. She was like another woman refusing to accept either advice or sympathy. Even the boy was now forgotten. But remembering the long previous strain to which she had been subjected, he forgave her. He realized the strength of her love, while he considered every available means for reaching the burning city at once. Finally he could no longer resist Isabel's mute pleading. Outside of professional obligation he seemed to see that she had suffered enough.

"I will go myself—find out where he is," he offered, impulsively. He stood looking down at Philip Barry's wife. "A special train for newspaper men leaves for the North to-night. I can go as a surgeon. I'll try my best to make you happy—as I promised to do," he humbly added. There was a lump in his throat and he went out. Isabel, stunned with gratitude, could not speak, could not thank him. But her face shone with the old courage of weeks back, lived through for Philip's sake.

The next day and the day after she went about the house as usual, thinking of others, trying not to brood. Reginald enjoyed his evening petting and in every way his mother seemed to be the same. Then gradually the late catastrophe became less fatal as time went by. For at last reliable news was beginning to come in from the ill-fated city, still burning, yet under absolute martial law. Thousands were now reported to be safe, though homeless, in the parks and upon higher, undamaged ground, beyond the region of flames. Relief trains had gone out on all the railroads; a few of them were now returning, packed with frightened, hungry refugees. And every one in the South seemed to be helping. The call for clothing for unfortunates had been answered generally. Isabel found strange comfort in sorting over her wardrobe, in giving useful parts of it away. Everything suitable for the dire occasion was gladly offered. Action restored her. In helping others she helped herself. Her generosity grew contagious throughout the household. Madame and the maids brought half-worn garments to swell the size of her own complete pile. Even thrifty Wing became duly exercised over the sad condition of countrymen driven from San Francisco's Chinatown. He talked incessantly of the prevalent heathen version of the earthquake, which involved the rage of an "old black cow" beneath the surface. One morning he rushed out of the kitchen in fresh excitement. A "cousin" from the North had just arrived, transported South in a cattle car filled with other celestials. Wing's face reflected the situation as he burst forth with the story of his friend's lucky escape. Isabel sitting alone encouraged him to speak.

"My cousin velly sad, now he lose he business—he so poor. What you think? Plaps I take him lectic car—go that Venice—all same dleam." Wing referred to a seaside resort nearby.

Mrs. Barry nodded. "You may have the day for your outing," she told him kindly. "One of the maids may take your place."

Wing beamed. "You velly good. I think I go—take my poor cousin—so he not be sad."

"An excellent plan," said Isabel.

He spread his hands with deprecating scorn for unwilling sacrifice. "I not help my fliend when he have bad luck, I no good!" he exclaimed. "Now my cousin begin all over—not one cent! He tell me all 'bout that earthquake, so terrible. He say, glound lock! lock! lock! all same ocean. Seventeen time! that old black cow kick up, under that gleat San Flancisco. That old cow never so mad udder time."

Isabel appreciated the heathen myth, but her soul sank as she thought of Philip. Where was he? Had he felt the awful shock, been hurt or killed in a wrecked hotel?

Wing went on. "Course I not b'leve 'bout that cow. Mission teacher say not so. I not know. I jus say mischief all done! Plaps old cow make trouble. Nobody know. Any old thing! I say, old black cow jus as good." A philosopher's pucker played on his lips and his strong white teeth parted in a smile. "My cousin horrible scare; cannot forget. He tell me,—all so happy, down that Chinatown fore that earthquake. He say people sit up late, go see flends; play domino; take little supper, len go bed. Everybody have heap fun. Nobody have fear! Pretty soon everybody wake up—hear that noise! be clazy? Old Chinatown be all same jag! Glound so dlunk, cannot keep still. Houses dlunk, too! plitty soon fall down. People no can stand up—no can see, all dark! Big noise come out sky; len fire make so blight. China loomans scleam! Little children cannot lun fast. Those priest up Jos House—no good. Everybody lun that bay. No use! Water mad too. Everything clazy! My poor cousin sick inside he heart; cannot forget."

"By all means take him to Venice," Isabel advised. And later she watched the pair go forth from the garden. Wing's vivid description of the catastrophe lived in her memory all day. But she tried to control herself; tried to believe that good news would soon come from Dr. Judkin. Then in the afternoon a messenger boy brought a despatch. She tore open the envelope, hardly daring to look within. But she nerved herself and read, "Your husband's manuscript accepted for magazine, also for book form." Philip's friend—the editor—had signed the golden message.

Chapter 35

Isabel held the telegram to her lips. She seemed to be kissing Philip. "Dear, dear husband, I knew, I knew," she softly murmured. The rest of the day she wandered about the garden, almost in an ecstacy of expectation. Something seemed to tell her that Philip was safe, that she would hear from him. But evening shadows fell without a personal word from the North. She was obliged to content herself by reading the evening papers, which were beginning to contradict certain overwhelming statements of days back. The hotel that had totally collapsed was now known to have been poorly built and was not the St. Francis, as formerly stated. Iron frames of many buildings had withstood the earthquake to go down at last before dynamite. Still, the list of dead and wounded would be a long one. Nothing could be definitely settled until after flames had ceased to lick through deserted streets. Suffering was intense on every side. Children had first seen the world under its open sky. Women, without beds to lie upon, had given birth in the open. Yet it seemed to be a time when the best part of human nature revealed a noble side. Already hope was beginning to stir in camps where ruined families clung lovingly together. Isabel's eyes grew moist as she read a thrilling story of heroism and courage.

Miss Lewis had gone back to the hotel, and when madame, complaining of a headache, kept her room, Isabel found herself alone. But one thought now absorbed her mind. Every moment she hoped for a telegram from Dr. Judkin. Then suddenly Wing again stood before her. He had returned from his day's outing and his countenance shone elate. Evidently he had fulfilled a purpose and brought new strength to the fainting heart of his unfortunate friend. As in the morning, Isabel encouraged him to talk.

"I come tell you—clause you so solly," he began. "Plitty soon I sure you hear you husbland—all safe! People say not so many kill, after all. Boss all light, I sure."

He tried to render sympathy and his attempt was not repulsed. "And you took your cousin to Venice?" Mrs. Barry kindly questioned.

Wing shrugged his shoulders and shook his head. He had lately cut off his cue, and now stood politely, with a gray "Fedora" hat in one hand. "Jus this way," he explained. "I decide—not take my cousin that Venice—all same dleam. Too much expense, I say. More better, not fool money, these hard time. I count up. Must spend two-dollar-half—go that seashore. Too much, I say. My poor cousin have no good shoe, no decent cloe, jus old thing—all tear. I say we not go foolish place after all. I tell my flend we stay Los Angeles—get cheap dinner, len go church. I say Plesbyterian Mission more better, not much expense. Too much sorrow, I say. No time go that Venice—all same dleam. Better hear 'bout heaven."

Mrs. Barry listened gravely. Wing gradually prepared his denouement.

"Plitty good time—all same business," he continued. "You see? My cousin have ole shoe—cannot las velly long. I jus take him that shoe store—see lindow—all so full."

"I understand," said Isabel. "You bought your friend a pair of shoes instead of taking him to Venice?"

Wing smiled. "All same yes," he qualified. "I find that shoe store—tell all 'bout my cousin. I say my poor cousin velly poor; have no shoe—claus he all bloke up that earthquake. That shoeman velly kind, give my flend fine Mellican shoe, light away—not take money. Len we go down street—tly get new hat. Big lindow so full! many nice hat—heap style. We stan long time, look in. Plitty soon man come out—smile, ask what we want. I say, 'My poor flend bloke up that earthquake; have no good hat.' Len man say, 'Come in get fit.' I say, 'No money.' Man say, 'All light; earthquake not come velly often.' My cousin so happy. After while he all fix up. New coat, new shirt,—everything all clean. Len we go down Chinatown, get dinner; go mission. Pleacher say heaven more better; not any earthquake—not any big fire. Pleacher say no old black cow kick up; so solly China people tell that story. Jus be good, he say. Be kind, help that sorrow up San Flancisco."

Isabel had listened throughout with keenest interest. At another time she might have found it difficult to control her countenance. To-night she could not laugh. Almost for the first time she realized the meaning of "the brotherhood of man." She found her purse and sent a liberal donation to celestials lately en route in the cattle car. "Relieve your friends as much as possible," she commanded. "You may take to-morrow off and spend the money as you see best. Those of us who can must help."

The simple kindness of her words fell clearly. Wing went out from her presence as one entrusted with a grave commission. She sat on with her thoughts.

Suddenly she was depressed beyond all control. Joined to her longing for Philip was the dread that he would never be able to forget that he had once been a Catholic and a priest of the Church. And she had made him forsake his calling. Again and again she repeated the publisher's telegram aloud. She tried to tell herself that when Philip came back he must see his way at once to go on with life. He would find his work appreciated, his book accepted. Then he would surely continue to write—become noted. Yet, perhaps authorship might not satisfy him. The man who formerly moved large audiences with his impassioned sermons might not after all make a success in literature. She recalled the first time that she had heard Philip address a congregation. His clear, eloquent handling of a great ethical subject had delighted her. Sitting in a pew with devout Catholics, she had been glad to forget the High Mass, which she did not understand, and follow the speaker in the pulpit. She had felt that her former lover, still her friend, had found his natural profession, for even before ordination, Philip—too young for a priest—was permitted to preach.

To-night Isabel's thoughts wandered back to an earlier Sunday in Venice—in St. Mark's—when they had gone together to vespers. Philip had then jestingly declared that but for her he would go into the Church. "I would like to preach at least one sermon as compelling as the one we have just heard," he told her, as they floated away in their gondola. Now his old words passed through her mind. A strange humility possessed her. Again she lived over those happy, youthful days in Venice. Still of all the churches abroad, of all the services she had witnessed, San Marco with the afternoon in question stood out, apart from other Romish background. At the time, Isabel caught a new view of the Catholic Church in Europe. For at midsummer vespers there had hardly been a suggestion of the pomp and ceremony which on stated occasions is supposed to make St. Mark turn over in his coffin, when clouds of incense pour through open doors into the piazza.

On that August evening all had been so simple—even without a vested choir. Informality prevailed throughout the humble audience. Every one moved his chair at will to the side of some friend. Women used their fans and whispered discreetly to one another. There were few "Sunday hats." Dark, uncovered heads and black crape shawls, richly fringed, worn corner wise, as only Venetian maids can wear them, discounted tawdry finery. Young men and little children sat on the pulpit steps. Every one sang from the heart. Wonderful Italian voices rose in natural harmony; then at last the patriarchal shepherd of the gathered flock came slowly forward. The beautiful old man wore no embroidered vestments on that summer's afternoon. Sheer, spotless white, showing but a line of scarlet beneath the lace around his hands, alone defined ecclesiastical rank. Yet he was strangely grand in the evening light of the golden church. A loving hush pervaded San Marco as he leaned over the pulpit, looking down upon his children. Isabel had never forgotten either the sermon or the marvelous voice of the speaker.

To-night it came to her that to be able to guide one's fellowmen to higher ideals through spoken words, was, after all, a God-given gift. And she had ruined Philip's opportunity. She asked herself a hard question. If he came back with his heart still turning to a natural calling, could she help him? At last she felt his inborn tendency; the early religious background which influenced his temperament. Things entirely outside of her own experience had always been vital to the man she loved. If he came back to her uncertain and wavering in view of returning health and implied difficult conditions, she must give him up. At last the situation seemed plain. But she was bitter withal. Philip's God was hard; she could not understand the miserable decision forced upon her as she sat alone.

Twice she tried to go above to bed, yet something held her. Hours wore on. She felt cold and started a fire. The heat from the hearth sent her into heavy, desperate slumber. She heard no sound. Philip entered softly and alone, for Dr. Judkin had hurried away.

AND AS HE WAITED—TRANSFIXED, he thought of that other night when he had stood outside the curtains, looking in at the woman he dared not touch. Then slowly Isabel opened her eyes, saw that her husband had come; felt that a miracle had restored his power to love. Renunciation of a dark hour was forgotten in a low, glad cry. Philip held her as never before. The strength of his arms made her dumb with joy. She could not speak. Her husband led her to the divan and she listened to his voice, his words. She heard him entreat her to forgive, to live anew.

She felt that nature's rending soul had tried their appealed case to enjoin his human need. Humility charged his fresh purpose as he tenderly pleaded for time to prove the revelation of terrible days back.

Later when she told him about the acceptance of his book he listened incredulously.

Suddenly he understood. "You kept it from deserved oblivion?" he said at last. A fond smile played on his lips. "What have you not done for me?" He kissed away her denial of all personal influence. "Take me back on trust," he implored. "I ask only for the stimulant of your faith; then perhaps—perhaps I may please you, do something worth while."

Isabel knew that his secularization had been sanctioned by The Higher Court. The years to come held glad significance for them both.

A Note About the Author

Mary Stewart Daggett (1856–1922) was an American author. Married to Charles Stewart Daggett, with whom she had three daughters and a son, her family settled in Pasadena, California in 1889. Mary wrote several novels, including *The Higher Court*, *The Yellow Angel*, *Mariposilla*, and *The Broad Aisle*. She also wrote plays, sketches, articles, poems and short stories. Set against the backdrop of a nation expanding as quickly as it was changing, Mary Stewart Daggett's works, which take place in the Midwest and California, explore themes of family, religion, obligation, and romance. Her characters face the onrush of modernity as they navigate the complexities of psychological and societal pressure, exhibiting a depth of emotion often disregarded in the fiction of today.

A Note from the Publisher

Spanning many genres, from non-fiction essays to literature classics to children's books and lyric poetry, Mint Edition books showcase the master works of our time in a modern new package. The text is freshly typeset, is clean and easy to read, and features a new note about the author in each volume. Many books also include exclusive new introductory material. Every book boasts a striking new cover, which makes it as appropriate for collecting as it is for gift giving. Mint Edition books are only printed when a reader orders them, so natural resources are not wasted. We're proud that our books are never manufactured in excess and exist only in the exact quantity they need to be read and enjoyed.

Discover more of your favorite classics with Bookfinity™.

- Track your reading with custom book lists.
- Get great book recommendations for your personalized Reader Type.
- Add reviews for your favorite books.
- AND MUCH MORE!

Visit **bookfinity.com** and take the fun Reader Type quiz to get started.

Enjoy our classic and modern companion pairings!

Printed in the USA
CPSIA information can be obtained
at www.ICGtesting.com
JSHW082357140824
68134JS00020B/2130